DANCE OF DEATH

"Check out the Lone Ranger over there," Joe said, laughing.

"I think he's a mariachi dancer," Frank said. "From what I've heard, it's really popular here."

Suddenly Joe's expression turned serious. "Maybe the guy didn't like that crack I made," he said in a low voice. "He's coming over here, and he doesn't seem too happy."

Frank saw that the masked dancer was only about six feet in front of them now. Through the mask's small holes, the man's eyes were chilling. This guy meant business.

"Hey, look," Frank began, "I'm sorry if my brother offended you, but—"

The mariachi dancer took another step toward him and Joe. He raised his hand, and sunlight glinted off something metallic. Frank's entire body tensed when he saw what it was.

"Joe, watch out!" he shouted. "He's got a knife!"

Nancy Drew & Hardy Boys SuperMysteries

Available from ARCHWAY Paperbacks

A NANCY DREW and HARDY BOYS SUPER·MYSTERY™

PASSPORT TO DANGER

Carolyn Keene

AN ARCHWAY PAPERBACK
Published by POCKET BOOKS
New York   London   Toronto   Sydney   Tokyo   Singapore

This book is a work of fiction. Names, characters, places and incidents are products of the author's imagination or are used fictitiously. Any resemblance to actual events or locales or persons, living or dead, is entirely coincidental.

AN ARCHWAY PAPERBACK *Original*

An Archway Paperback published by
POCKET BOOKS, a division of Simon & Schuster Inc.
1230 Avenue of the Americas, New York, NY 10020

ISBN: 0-671-78177-4

First Archway Paperback printing July 1994

10 9 8 7 6 5 4 3 2 1

NANCY DREW, THE HARDY BOYS, AN ARCHWAY PAPERBACK and colophon are registered trademarks of Simon & Schuster Inc.

A NANCY DREW AND HARDY BOYS SUPERMYSTERY is a trademark of Simon & Schuster Inc.

Cover art by Alfons Kiefer

Printed in the U.S.A.

IL 6+

PASSPORT TO DANGER

Chapter

One

"NANCY, STOP A SECOND, okay? I want to take a picture of you." Bess Marvin propped her sunglasses on top of her head, holding back her long blond hair. "Over there, so I can get that church in the background."

Nancy Drew grinned as she stood where Bess indicated. "Bess, we've only been in San Miguel de Allende for an hour, and already you've taken a whole roll of pictures."

"I can't help it. This place is gorgeous!" Bess snapped the picture, then flipped her sunglasses back down over her blue eyes. "Anyway, I promised George I'd take a lot, since she couldn't come to Mexico with us."

"It's too bad she came down with the flu," Nancy said. "I know she'd love it here."

She and Bess had paused at one side of the town's central square, which Nancy had learned was called el Jardín. It was dotted with carefully trimmed Indian laurel trees, and locals and tourists alike lounged on benches in the shade to escape the hot June sunshine. Around the square were hilly cobbled streets lined with stucco houses partially hidden by high walls. Bright purple bougainvillea and azaleas peeked over the walls, and the air was rich with the aroma of flowers and lemon trees.

"This is such a romantic place," Bess gushed. "I bet you wish Ned could be here."

Just the mention of her boyfriend's name made Nancy's heart skip a beat. "It *would* be nice," she admitted. "But he's got his summer job at the insurance company. Anyway, it's not as if this is a pleasure trip."

She suddenly remembered the three people who were waiting a few feet away. "Oh! I was so busy looking around that I almost forgot about the Obermans."

Helen and David Oberman had been friends of Nancy's aunt Eloise in New York City before they moved to San Miguel de Allende, Mexico, to open an art school seven years earlier. Nancy didn't know much about them or their nineteen-year-old daughter, Claire. All Eloise had said was that there was some sort of trouble at the art school and the Obermans needed Nancy's help.

"Sorry," Nancy said, hurrying over to the Obermans. "I'm afraid Bess and I are being hopeless tourists. All we've done so far is shop and go sightseeing."

Mrs. Oberman was a tall, slender woman in her forties. Her brown hair was cut short in a no-nonsense style that suited her tan shorts and white sleeveless blouse. "Don't be silly," she said with a warm smile. "We love to show off San Miguel. And as for shopping"—she pointed to the woven leather sandals Bess and Nancy had both bought in San Miguel's open-air market—"it's important to have comfortable shoes on these cobbled streets. Those huaraches are perfect."

"We're proud of San Miguel's beauty," Mr. Oberman added. He was the same height as his wife but stockier, with unruly russet hair and metal-framed glasses. "That's the main reason we decided to open our art school here. San Miguel was founded in the fifteen hundreds and was built up as a supply center for the silver mines in this area. A lot of wealthy mine owners built lavish homes here." He gestured to the elegant pink stone building complete with wrought-iron balconies across the street. "That was originally the mansion of one of them."

Claire rolled her bright green eyes. "Dad can't help making a lesson out of everything," she said, shaking her head. Her curly red hair bounced around her face. "But don't worry, I'll show you the fun things. We're going dancing tonight with Luis and—"

"Luis?" Mr. Oberman cut in, stiffening. "You know how your mother and I feel about him."

Claire shot him an icy glare. "You've made yourselves perfectly clear, but if you think—"

"Let's talk about this later," Mrs. Oberman cut in, with an embarrassed glance at Nancy and Bess.

Nancy could tell Bess felt as uncomfortable as she did. To change the subject, she said, "Maybe you could tell us more about why you wanted our help."

"Yes," Mrs. Oberman said gratefully. "I'm sure Eloise told you how hard we've worked to build up the Instituto San Miguel," she began. "We are open to both American students and students from the university at Guanajuato, the main city in the area. In fact, the institute is the largest English-speaking art school in Latin America."

"That's something to be proud of," Bess said.

"We are," Mr. Oberman said. "I just hope what's happening now doesn't ruin all the work we've put into the institute."

Mr. Oberman glanced around el Jardín to make sure no one was within hearing distance. Moving to a nearby bench, he gestured for the others to sit down while he paced in front of it. "A few days ago a janitor came to me with something he found behind a potted plant in the institute's cantina."

"What was it?" Nancy asked.

Mr. Oberman pulled a small card from his wallet and held it out for Nancy and Bess to see. Nancy took it and scrutinized it. The card was pale pink, with a blue heading that read Resident Alien, United States Department of Justice, Immigration and Naturalization Services. At the bottom of the card was a small white circle with a blue eagle inside it.

"This is what most people call a green card—it's

4

what foreigners need to live and work legally in the U.S.," Mr. Oberman explained. "The janitor found a pile of about a hundred of them."

"Actually, David and I are pretty sure they're *fake* green cards," Mrs. Oberman corrected. "We compared it to the valid green card of a friend of ours, and the colors were just different enough for us to think these cards were printed by forgers."

Nancy raised her eyes. "And you think someone is selling these to people who want to live and work in the States but can't do it legally?"

Mr. Oberman nodded. "Right. All they have to do is include a picture, a thumbprint, and their name and birth date. With a valid green card, a foreigner can enter and leave the U.S. as many times as he wants. Plus, he can work there legally. People will pay a thousand dollars or more for that chance."

"A hundred cards at, say, a thousand dollars apiece . . ." Nancy let out a whistle. "We're talking about a hundred thousand dollars!" She looked at the card one more time, then handed it to Mr. Oberman, who put it back in his wallet.

"At least. Helping people enter the States illegally is big business," Mrs. Oberman said. "Apart from buying phony papers, people will pay hundreds of dollars to a 'coyote'—a person who helps smuggle illegal aliens across the border. Every year thousands of people from Mexico and South America try to make the trip."

"Wow!" Bess exclaimed. "I guess they think it's worth it if they can make better lives for themselves."

"Yes. But unfortunately, many coyotes are more concerned with making money than with the welfare of the people who pay them," Mrs. Oberman said. "David and I have heard dozens of stories of people who were deserted along the route or led right into the arms of the border patrol."

"That's disgusting," Bess said.

"What's worse," Mr. Oberman said, "is that there's a good chance someone at the institute is involved. There's no shortage of artists who are talented enough to create a convincing fake. Plus, the blank cards *were* found on the institute grounds."

"You can understand why we're so upset," Mrs. Oberman added. "If it turns out that someone at the school is involved, the publicity would be very bad for enrollment. Hundreds of American students, including Claire, come here for summer school and transfer the credits they earn to their universities in the States."

Mrs. Oberman smiled at her daughter, but Claire didn't seem to notice. "Mom and Dad have made a great school," Claire said, leaning forward on the bench. "Too bad they're living in the Dark Ages when it comes to dating—"

"Claire—" Mr. Oberman began, but his wife put a hand on his arm to silence him. Then she continued speaking.

"Every year a panel of experts from Mexico and the U.S. visit to make sure the institute meets the academic requirements of both countries." She shook her head ruefully. "It's just our luck that this year's panel is to arrive next Tuesday."

"That's only five days from now!" Bess exclaimed. "It would be terrible if the school's reputation was ruined because of one person."

Mr. Oberman nodded. "That's why we came to you instead of contacting the police. I just hope you can find the culprit and resolve the situation quickly and quietly before the panel arrives and we have to contact the authorities."

"I'll do my best," Nancy promised. "Is there anyone you suspect?"

Mr. and Mrs. Oberman shared a quick glance. "We don't have any solid leads," Mr. Oberman said. "The only person we can think of is Maria Sandoval. About three months ago she took over running the cantina where the blank green cards were found. We thought someone who printed the cards might be using the cantina as a drop-off place. Maria hasn't done anything overtly suspicious, but—"

"She could be involved," Nancy finished. "I think we'd better start our investigation there."

Mr. Oberman glanced at his watch and sighed. "Good. Helen and I have a meeting now, but we'll see you back at our house for dinner."

"'Bye," Mrs. Oberman said, getting to her feet. "And thanks for everything, girls."

After Mr. and Mrs. Oberman left, Claire let out a huge sigh and turned to Nancy and Bess. "I thought they'd never leave!" she burst out. "As you probably noticed, Mom and Dad and I aren't exactly getting along."

Nancy just stared at Claire. She didn't seem to care at all about the fake green cards or the impact the crime could have on her parents' art school. "Umm," Nancy said hesitantly, "it was hard *not* to notice."

"The problem is that they totally hate my boyfriend, Luis," Claire said. "I finally meet a guy I'm crazy about, and they tell me they don't want me to go out with him! I mean, I feel awful about what they're going through, but that doesn't mean it's okay for them to tell me how to run my life."

Bess nodded sympathetically. "Did they say why they don't want you to date Luis?"

"They think I'm too young to be seriously involved. But I'm almost twenty, and if I want to keep on seeing Luis, I will." Claire's green eyes flashed with determination as she added, "In fact, we're even thinking of getting married."

"Wow! That's *so* romantic," Bess said.

"We've been dating for a month, ever since I got to San Miguel for summer vacation," Claire explained, her expression softening. "My parents don't think I should be so serious about him after so little time, but I know how I feel. The second I met Luis I knew we were meant for each other. You two can see for yourselves how great he is when you meet him tonight."

"I can't wait," Nancy said warmly.

"Too bad my parents aren't as enthusiastic about Luis as you two are," Claire said, frowning again.

In one way Nancy could understand how Claire felt. Nancy didn't know what *she'd* do if her father ever forbade her to see Ned. But a month didn't seem like much time to get to know someone. She didn't feel she knew Claire well enough to comment on it, though. "Maybe they'll ease up as they get to know Luis."

Then, changing the subject, she asked, "Do you think we could go to the cantina now?"

"Good idea," Bess agreed. "It's three-thirty, and I'm starving!"

Claire nodded. "I have my figure-drawing class at four, but I can show you where it is first," she said. "The cantina has great tacos. And you should definitely try a banana-mango *licuado*. It's kind of like a milkshake without ice cream."

Nancy and Bess followed Claire down one of the cobbled streets curving away from el Jardín. Nancy noticed the heavy wooden doors of the buildings they passed. All the doors had brass knockers. Over the tops of high garden walls, she caught glimpses of colorful, exotic flowers.

"Here's the institute," Claire announced ten minutes later, turning left into a wide, open doorway. "This property used to belong to one of those silver barons my dad was talking about. There are four different courtyards and about a dozen connecting buildings."

As soon as she turned into the entrance, Nancy fell in love with the Instituto San Miguel. The open courtyard was filled with flowers and greenery and flanked by elegant pink stone buildings. Through open windows, she could see students in classrooms.

"This place makes me want to take up painting immediately," Bess said. "It's beautiful!"

"That's the idea," Claire said. "Mom and Dad wanted the institute to be a school that would inspire creativity."

"I'd say they've done a pretty good job," Nancy commented as she followed Claire across the courtyard and around the side of another building. When they came to a second courtyard, Nancy and Bess stopped short.

"Oh! This is charming!" Bess exclaimed.

The courtyard was edged by a long arcade, adjoining the surrounding buildings. In the middle of the courtyard was a reflecting pool. A geometric metal sculpture had been installed at the pool's center. Lemon trees and ferns gave the courtyard a cool, shady feel and provided some privacy for the wrought-iron tables scattered about. Groups of students sat or stood around, eating, drinking, and talking.

The girls found a table by the arcade. As she sat down, Nancy's gaze was drawn to a part of the long arched building that had been closed off to form a kitchen and ordering counter. She noticed a short, middle-aged, heavyset woman behind the counter. Her graying black braids were twisted into a knot at the back of her head.

"Is that Maria Sandoval?" Nancy asked Claire.

Claire nodded. "That's her. Listen, I have to get to class, but I'll meet you two back here when it's over. Good luck!"

"I'm starving," Bess said, grabbing the plastic-coated menu that was stuck in a holder behind the salt, pepper, and hot sauce. "I think I'll have some *tacos de pollo* and one of those *licuados* Claire was talking about. How about you, Nan?"

Nancy turned her attention to the menu. "Hmm. Maybe I'll try one of these local specialties. The *sopa azteca* sounds good—tortilla soup with avocado and cheese—"

A deep, throaty man's voice coming from the covered arcade caught Nancy's attention. *"Cuándo puedo tener la tarjeta de residencia para los Estados Unidos?"*

"Tarjeta," Nancy echoed, frowning. "That's Spanish for 'card.' Bess, he's talking about getting a card for living in the U.S!"

"What?" Bess asked.

Nancy was too busy listening to the man to answer. *"Sí. La fuente en el parque Benito Juárez esta noche, a la medianoche. Está bien."*

"Bess, I think I just overheard someone making arrangements to buy a green card!"

Chapter

Two

"W HAT!" Bess scanned the cantina. "Who did you hear? Where?"

Nancy turned toward the arcade, but a column hid the person from view. "It sounded as if he was talking on the telephone over there." She jumped to her feet. "Wait here. I'll be right back."

A few quick strides took Nancy around the column into the arcade. A pay phone was there, but no one was using it.

She noticed that the arcade ended several feet ahead of her. A pathway ran next to it at an angle, leading away from the cantina.

Hurrying to the path, Nancy saw that it went to a building about fifty feet away. A flash of color there caught her attention. She saw a man with a dark ponytail and a colorful, woven shoulder bag disappear into the building. There was no other way in or out of this walkway, so she knew he had to be the guy who'd been talking on the phone.

"Hey, wait!" she called, but he didn't seem to hear her.

Nancy ran after him. She hurried through the building's entrance, but didn't see the man.

From the open foyer where she stood, hallways led in two directions, and a wide, curving stairway rose up to the second floor. It would be a waste of time trying to track the person down, she thought. There were too many routes he could have taken, and he could easily lose himself among the students.

Sighing, Nancy turned and headed back toward the cantina. In her mind, she went over all she'd heard the man say. He had mentioned something about going to a fountain in some park at midnight. Benito Juárez Park—that was the name of it. She would have to ask Claire where it was.

One thing was sure—when midnight came, she was going to be at that park, too.

The sound of Bess's animated voice broke into Nancy's thoughts. It never took Bess long to meet people, Nancy thought, smiling. She was probably surrounded by cute guys.

But when Nancy rounded the corner and saw who the cute guys were, she stopped dead.

"Frank and Joe Hardy!" she exclaimed. "What are *you* doing here?"

The two brothers turned toward Nancy. Both were handsome but in different ways. Eighteen-year-old Frank had dark, wavy hair, and at six foot one he was an inch taller and a little slimmer than his blond-haired seventeen-year-old brother. Frank was a little more serious than Joe, which appealed to Nancy. Joe flirted with every girl he met.

"We heard there were two incredibly cute girls from the Midwest here, so we flew down immediately," Joe said as he and Frank jogged over to give her hugs.

"You're as much of a shameless flirt as ever, Joe," Nancy said, ruffling his thick blond hair.

Frank twisted his brother's arms jokingly behind his back. "Just let me know if he's bothering you, and I'll deck him," he said teasingly.

Nancy laughed. Frank and Joe Hardy were the only two people she could think of who found mysteries as irresistible as she did. The three of them had teamed up on more than a few occasions.

"Are you two here on a case?" Nancy asked, lowering her voice. She glanced back at her table, where Bess was talking to a dark-haired boy and girl who appeared to be about eighteen.

"Nope. This is strictly a pleasure trip," Joe answered. The chairs at Nancy's table were all taken, so he grabbed one from nearby and pulled it over for Nancy. "Nancy, meet Ricardo and Rosa Perelis. They're twins, believe it or not."

Nancy saw right away that Ricardo and Rosa had the same big, yellow-brown eyes and tawny skin. "I believe it," she said. "Nice to meet you."

"Mucho gusto," Ricardo said, smiling at Nancy. "It's a pleasure meeting you and Bess."

Nancy noticed the special emphasis he placed on

Bess's name and the glimmer of interest in his eyes as he glanced at her. Judging by the flush on Bess's face, she was just as attracted to him.

"Mucho gusto," Rosa added. She was petite, with straight black hair cut in a pageboy and a yellow sleeveless minidress that set off her tanned skin. But whereas Ricardo seemed very energetic and lively, Rosa acted almost bored.

"You are from the Midwest?" she asked, gazing around the cantina.

Nancy nodded. "Near Chicago."

"Oh?" For the first time Nancy detected a glimmer of interest in the girl's eyes. "My boyfriend lived there before he came to San Miguel."

"Frank and I have been to Chicago a lot," Joe put in, dropping down in the chair next to Rosa.

While Joe launched into a story of a case he and Frank had solved in Chicago, Frank bent close to Nancy and whispered, "Joe's been trying to get Rosa to notice what a macho hunk he is since we got to San Miguel yesterday."

Nancy chuckled. "That figures. Any luck?"

"Not nearly as much as Ricardo is having with Bess," Frank whispered back. "Rosa keeps talking about her boyfriend, some American guy named Jim whom her father can't stand. Ricardo says that she rushes off to meet him every time her dad's back is turned—"

"Sounds familiar," Nancy said, thinking of Claire and Luis.

"Ugh! Frank, do you have to ruin a great afternoon by talking about my father?" Rosa had obviously overheard Frank and was glaring at him from across the table. "He does not need to know everything that I do," she said defiantly.

Joe shot Rosa a thousand-watt smile. "Hey, we totally understand."

"Do you?" Rosa jumped up from her chair. "Then you will understand why I want to see Jim right now. 'Bye. It was nice meeting you, Nancy and Bess." With a flip of her hand, she left the cantina.

"It is a good thing our father is in Mexico City," Ricardo commented. "He wants her to be more traditional, but—"

"That doesn't seem to be her style," Bess commented.

Frank turned to Nancy while the others were talking. "We're here on vacation," he said, "but what about you? What are *you* doing down here?"

Nancy hesitated, glancing at Ricardo. "We can talk about it later," she said, hedging.

Out of the corner of her eye, she saw Maria Sandoval heading their way. When the stout woman reached their table, she pulled a pad from her apron. *"Buenas tardes,"* she said. *"Qué desean?"*

After they had all ordered, Nancy smiled at Maria and said, "Your cantina is popular."

"Sí. Students, artists, people from the town— everyone likes Maria's cantina," she said proudly.

"Kind of like a mini-crossroads where Mexicans and Americans can get to know one another," Bess said. "If you ask me, we should have a school like this in the States where Mexicans can come to study."

Great! Nancy thought. Bess had provided her

with the perfect lead-in. "After all, it seems as if a lot of Mexicans want to visit the U.S.," she said casually.

The cantina owner's eyes narrowed for a brief instant before her expression became jovial once again. "Yes. The United States must be very interesting. Excuse me, but I have other customers," she said, flipping her pad to a new page.

Nancy watched the woman walk away. Was it her imagination, or had Maria reacted to her comment about Mexicans visiting the U.S.? There had to be a way to check her out.

Maria arrived soon after with their food, but Nancy was too preoccupied to eat much. She peeked into the open kitchen area behind the counter, but she didn't see any way she could nose around without being spotted. There had to be *some* place where Maria kept business papers and personal items.

"Maybe in there," she said softly to herself. A young man carrying a pile of clean aprons had just emerged from a closed door to the right of the kitchen.

Ricardo's voice cut into Nancy's thoughts. "What did you say?"

"Oh, nothing," Nancy mumbled. She was thinking of a plan to distract Maria when she noticed several men wheeling dollies loaded with boxes into the courtyard. Maria walked over to them and began inspecting the contents.

Here goes nothing! Nancy thought. Getting to her feet, she said, "I'll be right back. I'm just going to find the ladies' room."

She walked casually toward the counter. Once she was in the shadow of the curved archway, she hurried over to the door and slipped into the room, quickly closing the door behind her.

Nancy blinked a few times. Wherever she was didn't have any windows, but gradually some pale shapes emerged out of the darkness. She reached into her shoulder bag and pulled out her penlight. She flicked it on, and its beam picked out several rows of shelving piled with aprons, towels, pots, pans, and industrial-size jars and cans.

"A storeroom," Nancy murmured. She was about to start inspecting the shelves, when the beam of the flashlight fell on a colorful woven shawl hanging on a hook to the right of the door. With it was a worn leather shoulder bag. Could they be Maria's?

Nancy opened the handbag and shone her penlight inside. A change purse held a few coins, some crumpled-up peso notes, and a Mexican identification card with Maria's picture on it. The bag also held some tissues, a worn pocket Bible, and some keys tied together with string.

This isn't getting me anywhere, Nancy thought.

She was about to close the bag when something about the flap caught her eye. It was made of two pieces of leather sewn together, but a small section of stitching on one side had been undone. Nancy inserted a finger into the opening, then smiled as she touched what felt like a piece of cardboard.

Her heart was pounding as she carefully drew out a piece of folded paper. She cocked her head, listening for anyone approaching. Hearing nothing, she unfolded the paper and shone her penlight on it.

It was a road map of Mexico. Half a dozen routes had been outlined with colored markers. Some began as far south as Mexico City.

"And they all lead to the U.S. border!" Nancy whispered aloud. Her excitement shot a bolt of adrenaline through her.

"Incredible," she murmured, tracing a finger over the various routes that were marked. "Over half of these routes pass right through San Miguel!"

On the lower right-hand portion of the map, someone had made a few notations in ink: *Camiones—10/mes, Viajeros—120/mes, Tarjetas —50/mes.*

Nancy was pretty sure *camiones* were trucks, and *viajeros* were travelers. Could these figures mean that people were being smuggled across the border in trucks? If so, over a hundred people were crossing the border in a given month, not to mention the fifty cards. It looked as if this criminal ring could be huge!

Careful, Drew, Nancy cautioned herself. The language on the map wasn't very explicit—she knew it wouldn't hold up in court. She'd have to find concrete evidence linking the cantina's proprietress to the crime. If only she could—

Suddenly the doorknob rattled, and Nancy instinctively jumped. Her heart started racing. A split second later she heard Maria Sandoval rattling off a stream of Spanish words.

Nancy whirled around to face the storeroom door, flicking off her penlight at the same time. It sounded as if Maria was asking someone to help her unload the supplies in the storeroom!

Nancy's breath caught in her throat. Before she could even think about hiding, the door was opened, and a bright shaft of light streamed into the storeroom just inches from Nancy.

Any second Maria was going to walk in and catch her red-handed!

Chapter

Three

S EÑORA!" FRANK CALLED. *"Por favor!"* He wasn't sure what he was going to say, but he had to divert her attention. Because of the way Nancy had been acting, Frank decided that she must be in San Miguel on a case. So, ever since he'd seen her disappear into the room near the kitchen, he'd been keeping watch. He'd only turned away for a moment, to take a bite of his burrito. When he'd turned back, Maria Sandoval was talking to a helper and was halfway through the doorway.

"Sí?" Maria called back.

"We, uh, need help over here." He swung his hand and knocked over Joe's drink. It spilled all over the table and onto Joe's lap.

"Hey!" Joe jumped up and quickly wiped his jeans. "What was that for?"

Ignoring his brother, Frank gave Maria an imploring smile. "Gee, I guess I'm just a klutz. Sorry. Could you help us clean this up?"

Maria Sandoval frowned slightly. Frank wasn't sure she would come over. Finally she sighed, stepped away from the doorway, and went into the kitchen with her helper. Frank let out a big breath when he saw Nancy slip out of the same doorway a moment later.

"Very clever, big brother," Joe said sarcastically. "Next time, why don't you try spilling your own drink." Frank knew that Joe had seen Nancy and sized up the situation.

When Nancy returned to the table and sat down, she whispered, "Thanks for the quick save, Frank."

"Save? What are you talking about?" Ricardo asked.

Frank noticed Nancy hesitate. Before she could speak, Bess spoke up. "It's a case we're working on. Someone from the institute may be helping people cross the border into the U.S. illegally."

"A case? You are some kind of detective?" Ricardo asked, surprised.

Nancy nodded. "It's top secret," she put in quickly. "I'd appreciate it if you didn't say anything to anyone else."

Frank knew what Nancy was thinking. Anyone could be involved, even Ricardo or Rosa. "You can trust the Perelises," he assured her, clapping Ricardo on the shoulder.

"I won't say a word," Ricardo promised, "if Bess will promise to go out with me tonight."

Bess's cheeks turned bright red. "Actually, we're going dancing tonight with Claire—she's the girl we're staying with," she said. "Why don't you all come with us?"

"Sounds good," Joe said. "I wish we could stick around to help with the case, but we're going to Mexico City in the morning. That's where the Perelises' permanent home is. Ricardo and Rosa's father owns an art gallery there, and we've been invited to a big opening he's having tomorrow afternoon."

"The exhibit is called Máscaras de México— Masks of Mexico. They are pre-Columbians and were made by native Indians out of precious metals and stones before the Spanish colonized Mexico," Ricardo explained. "The masks are from private collectors. They are not for sale, but the publicity should generate a lot of business for my father."

"Wow. I can just picture all that gold and silver," Bess said. "Can you imagine what it must have been like to actually wear those masks?"

"I hate to burst your bubble, Bess, but the Aztecs lived a gruesome lifestyle in some ways," Frank said. "Some of their rituals included human sacrifice."

Bess grimaced. "Ugh! Do you have to say that while I'm still eating?"

"Sorry," Frank apologized. "Anyway, we've seen pictures of a few of the masks. They're pretty incredible."

"Mr. Oberman was talking about the exhibit during the drive here from the airport, remember, Bess?" Nancy said. "He received an invitation to the opening." Nancy turned to the others. "The Obermans are the people we're staying with."

Ricardo nodded. "Mr. Oberman and my father know each other. They're both experts in pre-Columbian art. They have a daughter, right?"

"Claire," Bess supplied. "She's the one we're going out with tonight. She's taking summer classes at the institute."

"Why don't you all come to Mexico City with us?" Ricardo suggested. "We'll have a great time!"

Frank could see that the girls were tempted—especially Bess. But he had a feeling he knew what their answer would be.

"Thanks, but we're here to work," Nancy said. "I wouldn't feel right about taking time off already."

"Nancy's right," Bess agreed. "But maybe we can get together after you get back from Mexico City."

Ricardo squeezed Bess's hand and stared intensely at her. "I would not miss that opportunity for anything."

"If Ricardo has anything to say about it, I

think our trip to Mexico City will be a short one!" Frank said.

"Benito Juárez Park? It's right near here, as a matter of fact," Claire told Nancy an hour later. She had returned just as the Hardys and Ricardo were leaving. Now she plucked a taco chip from the basket on the table, dipped it in salsa, and popped it into her mouth. "Mmm. These are delicious. Sometimes I think I would die without chips and salsa."

"I know what you mean," Bess said. "I must have eaten a ton of those this afternoon, not to mention all the tacos and *licuados*. I'll be a blimp by the time I get back to the States." Bess had a cute, curvaceous body, but she was always trying to lose five pounds.

Nancy, who was used to Bess complaining about her weight, smiled good-naturedly. "Bess, just enjoy it. We're going to be doing so much walking that you might even *lose* weight!"

"Promises, promises," Bess said, and reached for another chip.

Then Nancy and Bess filled Claire in on all that had happened while she was at class.

Claire looked at Nancy in awe. "I was only gone for about an hour, and you've already found the map routes *and* are hot on the trail of a green card buy. I'm impressed."

"On top of all that, Bess even had time to fall in love," Nancy added.

"With Ricardo?" Claire guessed. "I thought I

noticed him giving you a special look before he left."

"He is too cute! Not to mention really nice," Bess said. She grinned and reached for another taco chip. "Great food, gorgeous guys—so far, this has been the kind of investigation I like!"

Nancy leveled a serious gaze at Bess. "Actually, there's one more thing I'd like to do today if it's okay with you two," she said.

"What?" Bess asked.

"Even if Maria Sandoval is involved in the ring, we still don't know where they're getting the fake cards from. I'd like to check out any part of the institute where the cards could be printed."

Claire frowned for a moment, thinking. "We could look around in the photography studio. Maybe some photographic printmaking technique was used."

They paid their check, then Claire led Bess and Nancy to the building Nancy had gone into after overhearing the phone conversation. Now that Nancy wasn't in a hurry, she noticed the sculptures and drawings on display in the entrance area.

"Printmaking and photography are up there," Claire explained, pointing up a curved stairway. "The sculpture and jewelry departments are on the ground floor." She paused and looked at Bess and Nancy. "It's almost six, but Luis is probably still in the jewelry studio. Why don't we stop there first so you can meet him?"

Nancy was itching to get her investigation

moving, but she could see that Claire really wanted them to meet her boyfriend. "Sure," Nancy answered, smiling. "Let's see if this guy is as wonderful as you say."

"He definitely is." Claire headed to the left on the ground floor, following the corridor to the rear of the building. "This is the sculpture studio," she announced, turning into the last doorway. "The jewelry studio is beyond that arched doorway at the other end."

The sculpture studio was a long, open room. Its high ceilings, ornate moldings, and arched doorways were the only signs that the studio had once been part of an elegant mansion. Now the floor was splattered with clay, and pieces of metal and wood were piled everywhere. A few students were working, and Nancy could see a girl with a mask, apron, and blowtorch in the adjoining courtyard, welding two pieces of metal together.

"Here we are," Claire said, crossing the sculpture studio and leading the way through the arched doorway. This room was smaller than the sculpture studio and lined with worktables and shelves holding small tools and clear boxes containing stones and other materials.

"Oh, Luis isn't here," Claire said in a disappointed voice as she glanced around the room. "There's no point in sticking around here then. Let's go up to the photography—"

"Hi there, Claire!" a bright voice interrupted.

Nancy turned to see a man of medium height with shaggy brown hair, hazel eyes, and one of the most infectious smiles she had ever seen. His jeans and T-shirt had traces of clay on them.

"Hi, Sam," Claire said, smiling back. "Nancy, Bess, this is Sam Breslin, my sculpture teacher."

"Nice to meet you, Mr. Breslin," Nancy said.

"Call me Sam, please. We're on a first-name basis around here," the teacher said, shaking hands with Nancy and Bess. "Where's that boyfriend of yours, Claire? I commissioned the very talented Luis Diaz to make some silver fish for me. He said they'd be ready this afternoon."

Claire shrugged. "We were just looking for him, too. Are the fish for your new sculpture?" Turning to Nancy and Bess, she said, "Sam's sculptures are awesome. He uses all kinds of materials—clay, metal, rubber—"

"Old bolts I find on the street, bits of musical instruments that don't work anymore," Sam went on with a grin. "Everything but the kitchen sink. In fact, I *did* put a sink in one of my pieces."

Bess giggled. "Sounds interesting. I'd love to see your work."

"Come out to my studio any time," Sam invited. "Claire knows where it is."

"It's in the hills above town," Claire explained. "Maybe we can arrange for a visit sometime before—"

Glancing over Nancy's shoulder, she broke off, her face lighting up. "Luis!" Claire cried, rushing past Nancy with her arms open for a hug.

Nancy turned to greet Luis, but when she saw the guy who was standing in the doorway, her smile froze. There was no mistaking his striped shoulder bag or dark ponytail.

Luis was the person she had overheard arranging to buy a fake U.S. green card!

Chapter

Four

SURPRISED AND DISMAYED, Nancy glanced from Luis to Claire. How could she tell Claire that her boyfriend might be a criminal?

"Nan, didn't you hear Luis?" Bess's voice broke into Nancy's thoughts.

Forcing her attention back to the jewelry studio, Nancy saw that everyone was staring at her.

"Sorry. I was just, uh, thinking. What did you say, Luis?"

"I was just saying that I'm happy to meet you." Luis was quite handsome, with a high forehead and widely set dark eyes. His black cotton shirt was open at the neck, revealing a muscular chest. His face was filled with warmth as he gazed down at Claire, but Nancy thought she detected an underlying uneasiness. When Sam Breslin came over and put an arm around his shoulder, Luis practically jumped.

"I hate to interrupt," Sam said pleasantly, "but about those silver pieces—"

"Yes, of course," Luis said distractedly. "I finished them this morning." He led the sculptor over to a large wooden cabinet that was built into the wall and opened it to reveal a series of locked compartments.

"Isn't he terrific?" Claire whispered to Nancy and Bess. "He does really great work, too. Come and take a look."

Claire hurried over to the cabinet, but Nancy held Bess back. While Luis showed the silver pieces to Breslin, Nancy hurriedly told Bess that Luis was the man she'd overheard on the telephone.

"What!" Bess whispered. "Are you *sure?*"

Nancy nodded grimly. "Positive."

"Nancy, this is awful! What are we going to tell Claire?"

"Nothing for the moment," Nancy answered, letting out a sigh. "Let's wait until after we stake out the park tonight. In the meantime, with or without Claire, I want to check out the photography and printmaking studios."

"Good idea," Bess said. "Boy, I sure hope you're wrong about Luis. It would make things a lot simpler."

"That's for sure," Nancy agreed, but she had a feeling that solving the case was going to be anything but simple.

* * *

"What's wrong with this picture?" Joe grumbled to himself into his glass of soda later that evening.

He glanced across the table at Rosa Perelis. Colored lights from the dance floor strobed over the white sleeveless dress she wore and glinted in her yellow-brown eyes. The problem was definitely *not* her looks. It was that she didn't seem to realize that Joe was alive.

She had been sullen when they first arrived at the Laberintos nightclub to meet Nancy, Claire, Bess, and Claire's boyfriend. As soon as Jim Stanton arrived, Rosa had become happy. Now Nancy and Frank, Bess and Ricardo, and Claire and Luis were all on the dance floor. Just Joe, Rosa, and Jim were at the table, but Rosa was too busy with her boyfriend to include Joe in the conversation.

Joe shot a hooded glance at Jim Stanton. He isn't any taller than I am, Joe thought. And he's not in nearly as good shape. He looked okay in his snake-skin cowboy boots, black jeans, and cowboy shirt, but Joe didn't like the way his straight black hair kept falling over his eyes. It was as if he did it on purpose just so Rosa would reach over and brush it back for him.

Joe decided to try one more time to be friendly. "So, Jim, what do you do?" he yelled over the music.

"Jim's an artist," Rosa answered enthusiastically. "An abstract painter. He just sold a painting for a lot of money."

"Naturally," Joe grumbled under his breath. Then, more loudly, he asked, "Are you a student at the Instituto San Miguel?"

Jim shook his head. "Not anymore."

"Jim doesn't need classes," Rosa put in. "They're strictly for amateurs, right, Jim?"

Jim nodded but seemed distracted. He was barely paying attention to her. Joe had the feeling that he'd rather be anywhere else.

"Come on, Jim. I feel like dancing," Rosa urged, pulling his arm. Joe didn't think any guy could resist her beguiling smile, but Jim held back.

"Not now, Rosa," he said, frowning. "I've got some things on my mind."

Stanton turned away from Rosa and stared moodily around the dance club. He seemed so listless. What did a vivacious girl like Rosa see in him? Joe wondered.

This is where Joe Hardy steps in, he thought, "Hey, Rosa, want to dance?"

"Not now, Joe," she said, and turned back to her boyfriend. "Why don't you come to Mexico City with us tomorrow, Jim? I'll be so lonely without you. . . ."

Joe tuned out the rest of what she said and took a long swallow of soda, then scowled.

"Something wrong with your drink, Joe?" Nancy asked as she and Frank returned to the table. She sat down, fanning herself with one hand and taking a sip of her fruit drink with the other.

"The soda's fine," Joe murmured. "It's the company that's getting to me."

"Not this story again," Frank said, rolling his eyes. "I'm going to get something to drink while you bore Nancy with your love problems."

Nancy glanced across the table at Rosa and Jim

Stanton. "There are tons of cute girls here, Joe," she said quietly. "Why obsess over one who already has a boyfriend?"

Joe shrugged. "You're right. It's hopeless." He shot one more glance at Rosa. Then, turning back to Nancy, he saw her glance at her watch and gaze over at Bess and Ricardo on the dance floor.

"Come *on*, Bess," Nancy urged under her breath. "We've got to go."

"What's the matter? Are you two going to turn into pumpkins if you don't get home before midnight?" Joe asked.

"Not exactly," Nancy said. She lowered her voice. "We have to stake out a park near the institute. I'm pretty sure someone's going to buy a green card."

"Yeah?" Joe's interest was immediately piqued. "Listen, why don't I go with you? Bess is obviously busy, and those two"—he inclined his head in the direction of Rosa and Jim—"won't notice if I'm here or on Mars. Frank can keep them company."

Nancy laughed. "In that case, I accept. If Bess doesn't mind, that is. Let me just check with her, and then I'll meet you at the door. It's already twenty to twelve, so we should hurry."

While Nancy headed for the dance floor, Joe leaned across the table and tapped Rosa on her shoulder. "It's a little, uh, stuffy in here, so Nancy and I are going outside to get some air."

"Okay, see you soon," Rosa said without raising her eyes.

"Later, man," Jim Stanton added.

After intercepting Frank at the bar and telling

him where they were going, Joe met Nancy at the club's entrance. As they walked outside a cool evening breeze washed over Joe, helping to revive his spirits. Grinning at Nancy, he said, "Looks like it's you and me. *Dónde vamoose?*"

"If you're trying to ask where we're going, the word you're looking for is *vamos,* not *vamoose,*" Nancy said with a chuckle. "Claire told us that Benito Juárez Park is behind the institute." She looked up and down the street, getting her bearings. "We're pretty near the park, so we have to go a few blocks this way," she said, pointing down a hill.

The two of them started down the cobbled street, which was barely lit by heavy, cast-iron street-lamps. They passed groups of students, but the farther they went from the center of town, the more deserted the streets became.

"This must be it," Joe said about fifteen minutes later, eyeing the thick square of trees ahead of them.

Nancy paused in the shadow of the buildings at the end of the street and scanned the park. She saw few lights, and the paths leading from the street disappeared into a dark jumble of trees and shrubs.

"I don't see anyone here yet," Nancy whispered. "The guy I overheard said something about a fountain. Let's see if we can find one and hide near it."

"Sounds good."

Nancy and Joe crossed the street and slipped into the shadows of the park. They moved silently along the pathways, working their way toward the center. As Joe's eyes adjusted to the darkness, he saw the silhouette of a fountain about thirty feet ahead. Touching Nancy's elbow, he pointed.

"Great," she whispered, and ducked behind a bushy shrub to their right. "We'll be able to see both the street and the fountain from here."

Joe crouched next to her. For the next few minutes, they were watchfully quiet. The silence was so complete, Joe was almost afraid to breathe.

All at once he heard Nancy draw in her breath. A split second before he felt Nancy's elbow jab into his side, Joe spotted the figure. From the jerky way the man moved, glancing from side to side, Joe could tell he was nervous. He was keeping out of the light and wore some kind of hat pulled low over his forehead. Still, there was something familiar about him. . . .

"Hey, doesn't Claire's boyfriend have a ponytail?" he asked Nancy.

Nancy nodded. Then her eyes widened, and she pointed to Joe's left.

He turned in time to see a short, stocky figure crossing the street toward the park. As the person passed under a streetlight, Joe glimpsed short dark hair and a nose that had obviously been broken a few times.

"He looks like bad news," he whispered to Nancy. "I wouldn't want to run into him in a dark alley."

"Or in a deserted park," she whispered back. "He's heading for the fountain. Let's move closer."

Joe followed behind Nancy, keeping close to the trees. His body was tense, ready for action.

Some twenty-five feet ahead, the stocky man came to a halt beside the fountain, next to the man with the ponytail. In the darkness, Joe couldn't see either of them clearly, but he could hear them speaking rapidly in Spanish.

After a moment the man who had arrived first pulled an envelope from his pocket. Joe continued to creep forward. In another few feet he and Nancy would be in a perfect position—

Clunk! Joe felt the tip of his sneaker connect with a tin can, which clattered against a nearby tree trunk.

You idiot! his mind screamed. He and Nancy froze, but it was too late. The two men by the fountain had whirled in Joe and Nancy's direction. A split second later they took off in opposite directions.

Nancy and Joe both sprang into action. As Nancy sprinted after the taller man, she called over her shoulder, "Joe, take the other one!"

"You got it!" Joe was already on the stocky guy's trail, his sneakers pounding on the hard ground.

The man wound around trees, heading for the edge of the park, but Joe was gaining on him. By the time the man raced across the street—a flash beneath the streetlamp—Joe was only forty feet behind.

Up ahead the man shot into what looked like a dark, narrow alleyway. Joe reached the entrance to it just seconds later. He paused, the sound of his heavy breathing echoing off the buildings.

The alleyway seemed to stretch in front of him as

a tunnel of blackness. Joe couldn't see the stocky man, but he could hear his footsteps. In a flash Joe was after him again.

"It takes more than a dark alley to stop Joe Hardy," he muttered, breathing hard.

Up ahead he heard a metallic clunk, then the sound of a motor starting.

"What the—" Joe stopped short as a pair of bright headlights flicked on, blinding him. A second later he heard the grinding of a truck's gears. Then the driver gunned the engine and headed straight for Joe!

Frantic, Joe scanned both sides of him. The narrow alleyway was hemmed in by buildings on both sides. The large, hulking truck filled the entire width. There was no way Joe could get around it.

Whirling around, he headed back toward the alleyway's entrance at top speed, but he knew there was no way he'd make it. The truck would run him over in a matter of seconds!

Chapter

Five

JOE POUNDED TOWARD the end of the alley, running as fast as he could. He felt as if he were in a nightmare in which his legs were lead and could barely move at all. The roaring engine sounded as if it were right on top of him, and the truck's bright lights threw his desperate, flailing shadow on the cobblestones ahead.

Think, Hardy! he ordered himself.

Out of the corner of his eye, Joe spotted a doorway set into the wall, about ten yards ahead. If only he could make it there!

Joe mustered up every ounce of energy he could. The sound of the engine was so close now, it drowned out all his thoughts. Moving faster than he'd known he could, he flew forward, then dove the last few feet to the doorway.

Joe's shoulder thudded against the stone door frame. He didn't even have time to look up before the truck flew past him, its metal frame screeching against the building's stone wall and sending sparks into the air. A second later the truck roared out of the alleyway and disappeared.

For a moment all Joe could do was lean back against the door, gulping in air. When he finally jogged back to the park, Nancy was standing alone, across from the alley.

"Your guy got away, too, huh?" he asked, rubbing his sore shoulder.

Nancy nodded in the direction in which she'd chased the taller man. "There's a maze of alleys over there—he lost me right away. I got back here just in time to see that truck tear out of the alley. Are you all right?"

"Fine, considering that guy was trying to turn me into a hood ornament," Joe answered. In frustration he pounded a fist into his palm. "If I hadn't kicked that can, we probably would have had them both. Sorry, Nancy."

"Don't worry about it." Nancy was disappointed, but she didn't want to make Joe feel worse than he did. "The stakeout wasn't a total loss, anyway. When that truck drove by, I saw that it was blue and it had a name printed on it—Rápidex."

"Must be the name of a company. If you can track it down, maybe you'll find your connection to the phony green cards."

"That's what I was thinking, too," Nancy said. She took a pad from her purse and jotted down the name. "I'll ask Claire about it when we get back. She might not want to talk to me, though," she added. "Especially once I tell her the man I was chasing could have been Luis."

"I *thought* he looked like Luis. He must have left the club right after we did," Joe said. "It's touchy, but you'd better tell Claire. If I were dating someone who could be breaking the law, and one of my friends knew about it, I'd want to know."

"Me, too. I'm just not looking forward to it, that's all," Nancy said. "Come on. Let's go back. Maybe we're all wrong about Luis, and he's been at Laberintos the whole time."

The club was packed when Nancy and Joe returned. They had to squeeze through a wall of people to reach their table. When their friends came into sight, Nancy saw Claire sitting with Ricardo, Bess, Frank, Rosa, and Jim Stanton.

Nancy glanced at Joe. Luis was nowhere to be seen.

"You two were gone a long time," Rosa commented as Nancy and Joe sat down. "You must have gotten enough fresh air to last a lifetime."

"Anything interesting happen?" Bess chimed in.

Nancy knew Bess was really asking about their stakeout, but she didn't want to talk about it in front of everyone. "Nothing much," Nancy replied. Her voice casual, she asked, "Where's Luis?"

"He left soon after you two did," Claire answered. "He was really tired from working all day, so he went home to get some sleep."

Hmm! thought Nancy. Maybe the real reason he

left early didn't have anything to do with being tired. Could it be that he had made a detour to Benito Juárez Park before going home?

Nancy sighed. She couldn't put it off any longer. She had to talk to Claire about Luis as soon as possible.

"No, I don't believe it!" Claire cried, sitting down on her bed. "Luis would never buy a fake green card!"

Nancy and Bess had waited until they returned to the Obermans' and were ready for bed before telling Claire about their suspicions.

"I'm almost positive he's the one I overheard making a plan to pay for a card," Nancy maintained. She was sitting on Claire's rug with her oversize T-shirt pulled down over her knees.

"And the guy Nancy and Joe saw in the park tonight looked a lot like Luis," Bess added. "He could have access to the photography and print-making studios at the institute—"

"No!" Claire said. "Luis doesn't know anything about photography *or* printmaking. Besides, we checked out both those departments after we saw Luis, and there was nothing to show that anyone is making fake green cards. And believe me, I know Luis. He'd never do anything illegal."

"Not even for love?" Bess asked. "Maybe he's doing this to make sure you two can be together when you go back to the States in September."

"That doesn't make sense!" Claire said forcefully. "I could help him enter the country legally. If we get married, there won't be any problem."

42

Nancy didn't want to say what she was thinking —that Luis might be covering all his bases in case things with Claire didn't work out. If he *was* doing something illegal, marrying him was the worst thing Claire could do!

"This is all a mistake," Claire went on. "I promised Mom and Dad I wouldn't say anything to anyone about the case, but if I could just ask Luis, I'm sure he could clear everything up."

"Claire, you *can't* mention this to him," Nancy broke in urgently. "If word of our investigation gets out, the ringleaders could clear out and cover their trail."

Absently Claire smoothed her bedspread. "I hate lying to Luis—"

"Just keep quiet for a few days," Bess pleaded. "By then maybe we'll know for sure whether or not Luis is mixed up in this."

After a long, moody silence, Claire finally said, "Well, okay, but I don't like it."

"Thanks," Nancy said, feeling a wave of relief wash over her. "Oh—I almost forgot. The other man in the park was driving a truck with the name Rápidex printed on the side. Have you heard that name?"

"Sure," Claire said. "It's a trucking company that specializes in moving artwork. They're based in Mexico City, but a lot of people from San Miguel use them because they're the best in the business. It's cheaper than sending artwork by air. You can't really trust some of the small local companies, but with Rápidex you can be sure your artwork will arrive in the States in one piece."

"Back to the States, huh?" Nancy mused. "You know, artwork might not be the only thing Rápidex is moving across the border."

Bess's blue eyes widened in shock. "You think they're trucking illegal aliens across the border?"

"Of course!" Claire said excitedly. "You said that some of the routes on that map you found in the cantina started in Mexico City. Well, that's where the Rápidex office is."

"And a lot of them pass through San Miguel," Nancy added. "Someone here could be using the trucks as a cover to take illegal aliens across the border—or maybe drive them partway."

Bess frowned. "That makes sense, but how can we get proof?"

"We check out the Rápidex office, that's how," Nancy replied. She rose quickly to her feet and headed for the door of Claire's room. "I know it's late, but we need to call the Hardys. It looks as if we'll be going to Mexico City after all!"

Nancy gazed in awe at the powerful mural that stretched up over twelve feet in front of her. It depicted Aztecs being forced by Spanish *conquistadores* to work in Mexico's silver mines. The bold figures and earthy tones gave Nancy a strong sense of the cold greediness of the Spaniards and the cruel plight of the Aztecs.

"Wow," Bess said, standing next to Nancy. "It looks as if the Spanish totally devastated the Aztec culture."

"That's pretty much what happened," Claire said. "Right, Ricardo?"

Ricardo nodded. "Before Hernán Cortés arrived in Mexico, in 1519, the Aztecs had one of the most powerful, advanced societies in the world," he explained. "But between the Spanish guns and the diseases they brought, they wiped out almost the entire population."

He waved a hand, gesturing around the ornate stairway inside Mexico City's Palacio Nacional, where they were standing. "The artist Diego Rivera made these murals so that we Mexicans will not forget the good and the bad things in our past."

Early that morning the three girls and Ricardo had driven to Mexico City in the Obermans' second car, while Rosa and the Hardys took the Perelises' other car. Bess and Claire had convinced Nancy that their visit to Rápidex could wait until the afternoon so they could get a sneak preview of the exhibit of pre-Columbian masks in the morning.

"I'm glad we had some time to sightsee before meeting everyone at the gallery," Nancy said. "I wouldn't have wanted to miss this!"

Ricardo smiled. "I wish we had more time to look, but we must—how do you say it?—cut our visit short," he said, glancing at his watch. "It's nearly ten o'clock. My father will be waiting for us."

"Sure," Bess said, giving him a big smile.

The four teenagers stepped out of the National Palace and into Mexico City's hot, sticky air.

"That is the Zócalo," Ricardo said, pointing across the teeming Avenida Cinco de Mayo to the city's huge cement main square. "It's where the Aztecs' *teocali,* or Great Temple, once stood. Of

45

course, when Cortés took over, he completely destroyed it. We can come back to see some of the ruins later."

"Great," Bess said, continuing down the steps. "I can't wait to see the gold and silver masks at your dad's gallery, Ricardo."

"Some of the most valuable masks aren't gold *or* silver," Ricardo said. "The rarest one in the show is actually a jade mask made by the Mayans."

"Sounds great," Claire put in.

Ricardo led the three girls past the Zócalo and down the Avenida Madero. A few blocks down he stopped in front of an old stone building with a sign above the door that read Galería Perelis.

"Good," Ricardo said. "Here comes Papa with Rosa, Frank, and Joe."

Nancy had already spotted the Hardys and Rosa walking toward them. The man with them was about Nancy's height, but the straight, distinguished way he carried himself made him seem taller. He was impeccably dressed in a charcoal suit, his graying dark hair neatly trimmed.

"I am very pleased to meet any friends of Frank and Joe's," he said, a little formally. "I hope my son has been keeping you entertained?"

"Definitely," Bess said.

As Mr. Perelis turned to the gallery's entrance, Nancy noticed that the ornate glass and wrought-iron door was slightly ajar.

"Papa, you already opened the gallery?" Ricardo asked the question that had jumped into Nancy's mind.

"No. The gallery will be closed to the public until

the opening this afternoon," Mr. Perelis replied, frowning. "The guard, Juan Ramirez, was supposed to keep the front door locked and this alarm on"—he tapped a locked metal case to the right of the door—"until I arrived." He pulled open the door and strode purposefully inside. "I certainly will speak to Juan about this."

Nancy exchanged a worried look with the Hardys as she, Bess, and Claire followed the Perelises into the gallery.

Directly in front of them was a white reception counter backed by a tall wall panel with *Máscaras de México* printed on it in gold letters. Doorways on either side of the panel led to the open gallery space beyond.

"One moment," Mr. Perelis said, gesturing for the group to wait. "I will be right back."

After he disappeared through the left doorway, Rosa rolled her eyes. "I don't see why we should wait for him. Let's see the masks right away."

"Maybe we *should* go in there," Frank said, his gaze focused on the doorway to the main part of the gallery.

"I was thinking the same thing," Joe said. "If that door wasn't supposed to be open—"

"There could be trouble," Nancy finished.

Keeping her eyes peeled, Nancy stepped through one of the open doorways, then stopped short. Behind her, Bess drew in a sharp breath and murmured, "Amazing!"

The word didn't begin to do justice to the spectacular array of masks displayed in the open exhibition space. Silver, gold, and precious stones were winking at Nancy from every direction. In spite of her concern about the unlocked door, she was tempted to stop at each glass case.

"Aie!" Mr. Perelis's distressed cry interrupted Nancy's thoughts.

Nancy hurried to the rear of the gallery, where Mr. Perelis was bent over a man lying on the floor. The man was in a blue guard's uniform and rubbing the back of his head as he struggled to sit up.

"What happened?" Joe asked, coming up behind Nancy. The others also crowded around.

Mr. Perelis spoke urgently in Spanish to the man. Then the gallery owner jumped to his feet, his dark eyes searching the display cases.

"Papa!" Ricardo was pointing to his left.

Nancy gasped when she saw the empty glass case overturned on the floor. She had been so concerned about the guard that she hadn't noticed it or the empty pedestal next to the case until now.

"The jade mask," Mr. Perelis whispered, his face turning ashen. "It has been stolen!"

Chapter

Six

F RANK STARED AT the empty display case. "The jade mask—it's the most valuable piece in the show, right?"

"It is priceless!" Mr. Perelis grabbed a colored brochure from a nearby table and pointed at the mask on the cover. The photograph showed smooth pieces of jade fitted together in the whimsical shape of a monkey. Large hunks of turquoise studded the jade tail that wrapped around the outside of the mask.

"It is a very rare Mayan mask. There is no other like it in all of Mexico," Mr. Perelis went on in a distraught voice. "It took me weeks to convince the owner to let me exhibit the piece. What am I going to tell him now?"

Ricardo stepped over to his father. "Papa, we must call the police," he said urgently.

"Good idea," Frank said. While Mr. Perelis went into a back office, he and Joe helped Juan Ramirez to his feet. Soon after he was settled on a bench against the wall, Rosa appeared with an ice pack.

"Papa has a small refrigerator in his office," she explained.

The guard was pressing the ice pack to his head when Mr. Perelis returned. "The police will be here soon," he said. His smile was strained as he turned to Nancy, Claire, and Bess. "I am afraid I must ask you to leave. The police insist that nothing here be touched until they have examined it."

Ricardo stepped over to Bess. "I will go with you," he offered. "I can show you the National Museum of Anthropology—it is an amazing place. We will come back for the opening, and then all go out for dinner afterward."

It was just as well that Ricardo was so crazy about Bess, Frank reflected. The fewer people around, the easier it would be for him and Joe to look for clues.

"Will there still *be* an opening?" Bess asked Mr. Perelis, looking concerned.

"*Absolutamente,*" Mr. Perelis said angrily. "No thief will ruin the best exhibit I have ever had. I will not allow it."

"Papa, this thief is apparently one of the few people who does not pay attention to what you will or will not allow," Rosa said dryly.

Frank was surprised by the glint of satisfaction he saw in her amber eyes. Even if she didn't get along that well with her father. Frank would have thought she'd show a little more concern for what he was going through.

Apparently, Ricardo thought the same thing because he said something rapidly to her in Spanish. She clamped her mouth shut and crossed her arms over her chest. "I suppose I will go with you also, Ricardo, and leave Papa to his game of cops and robbers."

"Um, I guess we'll get going then," Nancy said quickly. Frank could tell she was trying to head off a confrontation between Rosa and her father.

As Nancy, Bess, Claire, Ricardo, and Rosa started for the door, Claire turned to Frank and Joe and asked, "Do you guys want to come with us?"

One look at Joe, and Frank knew his brother was thinking the same thing he was. "I think we'll pass. Joe and I might be able to help out here," he said.

"Okay. We'll meet you back here for the opening," Nancy said. Then she and the others left.

Joe glanced to where the guard was still sitting. In a low voice he said to Mr. Perelis, "As you know, Frank and I have done a lot of investigating. We'll be happy to help if you want."

Mr. Perelis shot a glance back and forth between Frank and Joe. "The police will be on the case, but—" He scowled. "They have not always had good luck in retrieving stolen works of art. If you are as talented as your father says, I could use the help," he said.

"These are just two boys," the guard said in heavily accented English.

Frank frowned as he turned to the guard, who

had gotten up from the bench and was now standing next to them, the ice pack pressed to his head. For the first time, Frank noticed Ramirez's quasimilitary appearance. His dark hair was cut very short, and his expression was tough. His uniform enhanced his solid, muscular build.

"For your information," Joe said, "Frank and I have solved crimes that not even the police—"

"Chill out, Joe." Frank interrupted. It was bad enough that Ramirez knew they were investigating, but alienating the guy wasn't going to help.

"Why don't you start over again and tell us everything that happened," Mr. Perelis said. "In English, so Frank and Joe can understand."

The guard remained stubbornly silent for a moment. Then he walked back to the bench against the gallery wall and sat down. "I arrived here this morning at six o'clock to relieve Gerardo—"

"The night guard," Mr. Perelis explained to Frank and Joe. He paced back and forth in front of the guard, his hands linked behind his back.

Ramirez nodded. "After letting Gerardo out, I locked the door. Gerardo had turned off the alarm to let me in, so I went to reactivate it."

"That's the metal box outside the entrance?" Frank asked.

"Yes. There is a second box here inside the gallery, so that the alarm can be turned on and off from outside and inside," Mr. Perelis explained. "Only the guards and I have keys to the boxes."

As he spoke, Mr. Perelis led the Hardys to a recessed area to the right of the entrance. Set into the alcove was a stainless steel box.

"The lock hasn't been tampered with," Frank commented, leaning over Joe's shoulder.

"The reason for that is simple," Ramirez said disdainfully. "I did not have time to turn the alarm back on. Before I could—" He gestured with his ice pack, tapping himself on the back of the head.

"You were knocked out," Frank finished. "And when you regained consciousness, the mask was gone."

The guard gave a small nod. "You are truly a brilliant detective."

Frank ignored the sarcasm in Ramirez's voice. "I take it you didn't see the thief?"

"No, I did not," Juan Ramirez answered.

"There is a separate alarm for the exhibition cases," Mr. Perelis explained, leading Frank and Joe to the rear of the gallery, where there was another locked case. "It does not appear to have been tampered with, either."

"An experienced thief could open it by using a lock-picking kit and not leave any signs of disturbance," Joe pointed out. "From the looks of things, we're dealing with a pro here."

Ignoring Frank and Joe, the guard turned to Mr. Perelis. "This is my fault. I am sorry, señor."

Mr. Perelis stepped over to the guard, his expression softening. "Do not blame yourself, Juan. You could have been seriously hurt. In fact, why don't you take the rest of the day off? I can call one of the other guards—"

"I'm fine," the guard insisted. "I would not feel right leaving before the opening is over, especially after what has happened—"

As he continued to talk about security for the opening, Frank stepped a few feet away and gestured for Joe to follow. "This guy's a real prince," Frank whispered. "I know he was knocked out, but—"

"He didn't exactly give us the warmest welcome in the world," Joe finished, shaking his head in disgust. "Are you thinking what I'm thinking?"

Frank nodded. "This may have been an inside job," he whispered. "We'll have to talk to the night guard, too. I don't know—Ramirez *was* knocked out, but I don't like the guy's attitude. It's possible that he's involved in some way."

"Whoever stole that mask must have left some clues," Joe muttered. "Let's check the place out." They agreed to start with the case where the jade mask had been displayed.

The case consisted of a three-foot-square stone pedestal and the heavy glass cover that was now overturned on the floor. There were electronic sensors at all four corners of the stone base. Frank knew that the glass case was supposed to rest on the sensors, which were rigged to set off the alarm if the case was removed.

The base looked clean, so Frank and Joe both knelt down to examine the overturned case.

"Wait a minute," Frank murmured. "This sucker is huge!"

"Not to mention the glass is at least a half-inch thick," Joe added. "It must weigh a ton."

"One person couldn't possibly lift this case alone," Frank said, thinking out loud. "Two people, at least, must have been in on the heist."

"Frank, check this out!" Joe called, dropping to the floor.

Frank was next to him in an instant. On the floor in front of them was a small, flat tin ornament in the shape of a hand. "That's weird. Hey, Mr. Perelis!" he called. "Can you take a look at something?"

Mr. Perelis and Juan Ramirez hurried over. When he saw the ornament on the floor, the gallery owner gasped. "It is as I feared," he said, covering his face with his hands.

Frank and Joe were confused. "What are you talking about?" Joe asked the gallery owner.

"When I mentioned that the police have not always had luck solving art thefts, I did not tell you the complete story," Mr. Perelis began. "In the past year, there have been some major unsolved art thefts—a Matisse painting from a private collection in Paris, a golden necklace from an Egyptian tomb—"

"I read about that," Frank put in. "You think the same guy stole the jade mask from here?"

"I do," Mr. Perelis replied. "Each time the thief left a small glove or hand. It was his calling card. It was kept out of the newspapers, but I heard about it from associates in the art business."

Joe let his breath out in a rush. "I've heard of thieves using gloves as calling cards before. It's kind of like saying they have the perfect touch and can't be caught." When Mr. Perelis nodded, Joe said, "But I don't get why this guy steals such well-known stuff. I mean, anyone who knows anything about art would know the jade mask was stolen, right? Who'd buy it?"

"Not everyone is ethical," Mr. Perelis said. "There are unscrupulous collectors who would pay a fortune to secretly own a masterpiece such as the jade mask. I have heard rumors that the Matisse painting went to a wealthy collector in Japan, though it has never been proven.

"Everyone in the art community knows that this thief is a master at what he does," Mr. Perelis went on angrily. "The police will not be able to recover the mask, and no collector will ever trust me with his artwork again."

"On the other hand, whoever stole the jade mask has never tangled with the Hardys before," Joe said with a cocky grin.

"I am sure he will be terrified," Juan scoffed.

Frank was getting sick of the guard's insults, but he didn't want to antagonize him. He and Joe needed the man's cooperation. Turning to Mr. Perelis, Frank said, "We'll do our best to catch the thief." He looked down at the ornament. "I'm sure the police will dust the ornament for fingerprints, but I doubt they'll find any. In the meantime, we can start by tracking down the manufacturer of the hand."

Also by keeping an eye on Juan Ramirez, he added to himself.

"I feel underdressed," Bess said that evening, plucking at the white open-weave sweater she wore over her sleeveless red blouse and white cotton skirt. She, Nancy, Ricardo, and Rosa were standing next to the refreshment bar that had been set up for the opening of the Máscaras de México show.

"I know what you mean." Nancy glanced down at the turquoise sundress she wore. It was the perfect traveling dress, but it seemed drab in comparison to the sparkling cocktail dresses the women were wearing.

"Anyway, I'm glad we're here," Bess added. "After visiting the Aztec ruins by the Zócalo and going to the anthropology museum, I feel as if I know a little more about the people who made all these masks. They sure are beautiful."

Apparently, a lot of other people thought so, too. It seemed to Nancy that just about all of Mexico City had shown up for the opening. Frank was circulating, watchfully alert as he regarded the crowd. Joe had posted himself by the door, while Juan Ramirez was standing at the rear of the gallery.

"There are many beautiful Mexican arts and crafts," Ricardo said proudly. "You will see tomorrow, when we visit the Bazar Sábado, Mexico City's crafts fair."

Nancy nodded distractedly, but her attention was elsewhere. "I feel sorry for your dad," Nancy said as her gaze fell on the older man. Across the room, Mr. Perelis was talking to a gray-haired couple. His smile didn't hide the tension in his face.

Ricardo nodded and let out a sigh. "It's bad enough that the jade mask was stolen, but the reporters are driving him crazy." A camera's flash went off just then, as if to illustrate his point. "They have been hounding him."

"Oh, they are keeping things interesting, that is all," Rosa said lightly. She took a sip of her soda as she scanned the room. "Since Jim could not be here, at least *something* fun is happening."

Nancy shot Rosa a sideways look, but before she could say anything, Claire and her parents appeared next to them.

"Hello," Mr. Oberman greeted the group. "Claire just told us about the theft. What a terrible blow to the art world."

"It certainly is," Mrs. Oberman added. "Do the police have any leads?"

Nancy wasn't sure how much to reveal, so she just said, "They spent the afternoon here. I'm sure they're doing everything they—"

She broke off as her gaze fell on Ricardo. His entire body had stiffened, and his attention was focused on the gallery's entrance.

"Ricardo, what's wrong?" Nancy asked.

He didn't appear to have heard her. "Uh-oh," Ricardo mumbled. *"Es un gran problema."*

"Huh?" Bess looked at Ricardo in confusion.

"Sounds as if there's a problem," Nancy said. She turned toward the entrance, and her gaze fell on one of the tallest men she had ever seen. He had wavy blond hair, a pale complexion, and blue eyes that danced with amusement as he looked around the gallery. He was wearing an expensive linen suit.

"Who's that guy?" Bess asked.

"That's Quentin Cole," Mr. Oberman answered, following the girls' gaze. "He's a well-known art collector from England."

Ricardo's eyes were still glued on the man. "I

must get him out of here—quickly. If my father sees him, there will be terrible trouble."

"I don't get it," Bess said. "What's the big deal about—"

She broke off as Mr. Perelis stormed to the front of the gallery.

"You!" Mr. Perelis's face was purple with rage as he stopped in front of the tall blond man. "How dare you show your face in my gallery. You dirty thief! I'll show you—"

Nancy watched in horror as, without another word, Mr. Perelis punched Quentin Cole in the face.

Chapter

Seven

"WHOA!" Joe had been just a few yards from the gallery entrance when he saw Mr. Perelis storm over to the tall, slick-looking man. Now the man had blood dripping from his nose and down the front of his suit, and Mr. Perelis looked as if he was winding up to take another shot.

Joe sprinted forward, elbowing his way between two older women in evening gowns. "Frank, quick!" he called over his shoulder.

He stepped between the two men and grabbed Mr. Perelis's arm before he could punch the other man again. "Hey, calm down, Mr. P. What's going on?"

Out of the corner of his eye, Joe saw Frank go over to the man with the bloody nose. The crowd around the two men had erupted in exclamations.

Within seconds Juan Ramirez materialized next to Mr. Perelis. "I will take over here," he told Joe.

Joe quickly turned his attention to the crowd. "Okay, okay, calm down, everyone," he said. "Everything is fine. Please, just continue to have a good time." To his relief, Ricardo followed his lead, smiling calmly and speaking in Spanish. The crowd began to disperse.

Photographers snapped pictures by the dozen. Turning to Mr. Perelis, Joe saw the gallery owner blink into the bright lights. His fury quickly faded.

"Please go back to what you were doing." Mr. Perelis gave a forced smile. "This is nothing."

While Juan Ramirez firmly herded the reporters and photographers out the door, Mr. Perelis turned back briefly to the tall blond man.

"Get out of my gallery," he muttered through his smile. Then he turned away and went over to a couple and started talking to them as if nothing had happened.

"Are you all right, Mr—?" Frank asked the man Mr. Perelis had punched.

"Cole. Quentin Cole," the man answered in a crisp British accent. He had taken a handkerchief from his jacket pocket and was holding it to his nose. Joe couldn't believe it, but Cole was actually smiling.

"Maybe you'd better tell us what that was all about," Joe suggested.

Quentin Cole's eyes didn't lose their amused gleam. "Yes, I'm sure you'd like that." Then, with a cryptic smile, he turned away from the Hardys and stepped casually over to the refreshment table.

What was with this guy? Joe wondered.

"You heard what Mr. Perelis said," Frank murmured quietly. "You'd better get out of here."

Joe was about to head after Cole when Rosa spoke up next to him. "I see you've met the famous Quentin Cole," she said. "He has a way of livening things up, don't you think?"

"You mean a way of wrecking the biggest event in your dad's career," Joe said. He gave Rosa a quizzical look. "Doesn't that bother you?" he asked, but her only answer was to make a face he couldn't quite read.

"What's that guy's story, anyway?" Frank asked Rosa. "Why does your dad hate him so much?"

"Oh, everyone knows about Quentin Cole," Rosa said. "The trouble is, no one has ever been able to catch him with red on his hands—is that how you say it?"

"Red-handed," Joe corrected. "You mean, *that's* the guy your dad and Ramirez told us about?" he asked. "The thief who leaves a calling card but not enough evidence to be convicted?"

"Yes," Rosa said. "There is no proof but—"

"He's pretty arrogant, too, if he has the nerve to show up here after stealing the jade mask," Frank put in. "No wonder your father socked him—"

Suddenly he grabbed Joe's arm. "Hey, don't look now, but our guy is leaving," Frank said urgently.

As Quentin Cole walked smoothly toward the gallery door, Joe moved automatically to follow him.

"One of us should stay here," Frank pointed out.

"We promised Mr. Perelis we'd keep an eye on things."

"I can go with you, Frank," Rosa said. "I have a moped, so we can be sure of keeping up with him." She grabbed Frank's hand and pulled him toward the door.

The two of them were outside before Joe had time to object. For some reason, it made him nervous to have Rosa involved. Up until now, she'd acted almost pleased to see her father in trouble. Joe wasn't sure that she could be counted on to really help out.

"Do you know this gallery?" Frank leaned forward on the moped to read the name on the gallery's awning.

"Yes, I know it," Rosa answered. "It specializes in pre-Columbian art."

"It's the third place Cole's gone into," Frank said. He looked around the side of the car they were parked behind and tried to see through the gallery's large window. All he saw, however, was the sun's glare bouncing back at him. He made a mental note of the name and location of the gallery so that he and Joe could come back later and check it out.

"There must be some reason he's making the rounds of dealers," he murmured, thinking out loud. "Maybe he's making plans to sell the jade mask."

Rosa shrugged. "Maybe." She turned around on the moped seat to look at Frank. "Do you think that I am a terrible daughter?"

The question took Frank by surprise. "Uh, I guess I don't really understand why you keep putting your dad down when it's obvious that he's so upset about the jade mask being stolen," he hedged.

"I know what happened to him is terrible," Rosa said, letting out a sigh. "But I cannot seem to help always being in a battle with him. It has been this way since I met Jim last year."

"Why does your dad hate Jim so much?"

"He thinks that Jim is only interested in me because of my family's connections in the art community," Rosa said.

Frank wasn't sure what to say. He had only met Stanton once, at the dance club in San Miguel. The guy hadn't seemed very interested in Rosa's art connections or in anything else, either. He hadn't said much of anything, in fact.

"I don't know Jim very well," Frank hedged. "What makes your dad think that—"

Frank broke off as his gaze landed on a person walking by. "Hey, that's Cole! I completely missed seeing him leave that place. Come on," he said urgently. "Let's stay on top of him."

Brilliant detective work, Frank chastised himself as Rosa started her moped and followed Cole at a discreet distance. The guy could have walked right in front of us and you wouldn't have seen him.

"No more distractions, okay?" he said to Rosa.

For the next half hour they hardly said a word; they just watched. Quentin Cole simply wandered in and out of galleries.

"I'm going to move in a little closer on foot," Frank said after Cole had gone into yet another place, the Galería Santos. "I want to see what he's up to."

Frank hopped off the back of the moped and jogged toward the gallery window. The sun had sunk below the buildings, and without the glare, he thought he might be able to see inside.

He was just ten feet from the gallery when the door opened again and Quentin Cole emerged. For the briefest moment Cole's gaze flicked over Frank. Then, without showing any signs of recognizing Frank, Cole strolled to the curb and waved for a taxi. He didn't seem to be in a hurry as he got in, but a moment later the cab screeched away from the curb and into the heavy traffic.

"Rosa, don't lose that cab!" Frank called, racing back to the moped and hopping on.

She roared after it, and Frank had to grab her waist to keep from being thrown off the moped. "Yikes!" he cried as she squeezed between a truck and car, with just inches to spare on either side.

"Is something the matter?" Rosa called back over the deafening roar of the motor. "Should I slow down?"

"No! We have to catch up with him!"

Rosa hit the gas. They seemed to be on a crash course with half the cars, trucks, and buses around them, but Frank couldn't worry about that. Every ounce of his attention was focused on the yellow taxi about half a dozen cars ahead of them.

Rosa drove into a traffic circle, cutting in front of

a tour bus. "Yee-ha!" Frank yelled as the bus's horn blared behind him. "Way to go, Rosa!"

Cars jumped from lane to lane without any warning, but Rosa wove expertly among them. Frank could sense her concentration as she pushed the moped to the limit.

Now they were on a broad, straight avenue flanked by ornate colonial mansions on one side and high-tech glass-fronted buildings on the other.

"Another traffic circle," Rosa yelled to Frank over her shoulder as they approached a second circle. "This street—the Paseo de la Reforma—is full of them. We will catch up to him here."

Frank tightened his grip on her waist as she entered the circle. There was just one car between them and Quentin Cole's taxi now. Cars and motorcycles entered the circle from side roads, but Rosa determinedly inched closer to the taxi.

"Yes!" Frank cried as she pulled ahead of the car. He flailed a fist at the taxi, which was just a few yards in front of them. "We've got you now—"

Frank broke off as he caught sight of a flash of gold to the right, just ahead of them. "What—?"

Pulling onto the circle right in front of them was a gold, pumpkin-shaped carriage. The open carriage was decorated with flowers, and inside sat a woman in a white bridal gown and a man in a tuxedo.

What is this, Frank wondered, Cinderella goes to Mexico?

The thought flashed through Frank's mind and was immediately followed by the realization that Rosa hadn't yet spotted the carriage.

"Rosa, stop!" he screamed. The carriage was just a few feet in front of them.

"Aie!" Rosa's desperate cry filled the air. She jammed on the brakes and tried to veer left around the carriage, but the busy traffic left no room.

In a second they were going to crash into the bride and groom!

Chapter

Eight

BRACE YOURSELF!" Frank cried. He gritted his teeth and held tighter to Rosa as the moped's front tire struck the carriage. The ear-splitting screech of metal on metal ripped through the air, and Frank felt himself being thrown up and off the moped.

The sounds of terrified screams, shrieking brakes, and blaring horns erupted all around them. Frank barely had time to cover his head with his arms before he thudded against the carriage, then somersaulted and fell against someone. His hands caught in a gauzy material. When he looked up, he saw that he was sitting in the bride's lap, staring right into her wide, startled eyes.

"Oomph!" Rosa's breathless exclamation sounded from nearby. She was lying at the groom's feet, her legs splayed across the floor of the carriage.

Traffic around them had completely stopped, and people crowded around the carriage, exclaiming in Spanish. Frank spotted Rosa's moped lying on its side a few yards from the carriage, its front wheel twisted like a pretzel.

"Rosa, are you all right?" he asked, trying to catch his breath.

Rosa struggled to a sitting position. "Better than these two," she said. She nodded toward the bride and groom and began to giggle. "Frank, I think the groom is starting to get jealous."

Seeing the glowering expression on the groom's face, Frank realized with a start that he was still sitting in the bride's lap. The woman's face was as white as her dress. She hadn't said a word but just kept staring at him, as if in complete shock.

He extricated himself from the wedding gown. "Sorry to, um, drop in on you like this," he quipped. "I mean, sorry to crash and run, but we've got to get out of here. Come on, Rosa!"

Frank grabbed Rosa's hand, jumped from the carriage, and elbowed through the crowd. He stared down the Paseo de la Reforma, but there was no telling which, if any, of the many yellow taxis was the one they had been chasing.

Quentin Cole had gotten away.

"Thanks for coming to the Rápidex office with me, Claire," Nancy said, staring at the stylized blue *R* on the sign in front of her. "I hope you didn't mind leaving the opening early, but if we want to find out who's selling fake green cards before Tuesday when that educational panel comes to check out the institute, I really don't think we should put off this visit any longer."

Earlier that afternoon, the girls' trip to the Museum of Anthropology had been so fascinating that they'd lingered longer than Nancy had intended, and it was too late to make the trip to Rápidex before the art opening.

"No problem," Claire said. "I got to see all the masks *and* all the excitement when Quentin Cole showed up." She looked around the deserted industrialized area. "Besides, this isn't exactly a tourist spot. I'm glad you didn't come here by yourself."

"Me, too," Nancy admitted. "I could tell that Bess wanted to come with us, but I didn't want to attract attention with a group. Anyway, when I told them where we were going, Ricardo and Joe seemed grateful that Bess could help them at the gallery."

Claire nodded. "Especially since Frank and Rosa took off after Quentin Cole. There sure is a lot going on! I'm glad we're all meeting for a late dinner after the opening, so we can fill one another in."

Nancy glanced at her watch, then said, "It's already after seven. It's a good thing businesses here stay open longer than they do in the States."

"Most places close for a siesta between two and five, but then they stay open until eight o'clock or so," Claire explained. Glancing at the Rápidex building, she asked, "So what's our plan?"

"Well, we don't know if it's a customer or someone who works for the company who tried to run down Joe," Nancy said, "so we can't just prance in there and tell them we think their trucks are being used to transport illegal aliens across the border.

Let's see if we can get a look at their records. If they have a client from San Miguel—"

"Like maybe Maria Sandoval?" Claire asked.

"Or anyone else from San Miguel who rents trucks from them regularly."

Claire bit her lip. "But what if the person who's smuggling illegal aliens works for Rápidex? He could be doctoring the records or even taking the trucks without leaving any paper trail."

"That's true," Nancy said. "We'll have to keep our eyes open for anything that doesn't seem right. Follow my lead, okay?"

Nancy opened the door, and she and Claire went into the office. Inside was a long counter with colorful Rápidex brochures on it. A heavyset woman wearing a blue smock stood at a computer station behind the counter. A door in the wall behind her was open, revealing a garage area filled with trucks.

"Buenas tardes. Puedo ayudarle?" the woman asked, a smile on her round face.

"Do you speak English?" Nancy asked.

"Yes, of course," the woman answered smoothly. "Many of our customers are Americans."

Some of them might be crooks, too, Nancy thought. "We're artists who are spending the summer in San Miguel de Allende," she said aloud, making up her story as she went along. "We'll need to truck several large works of art back to the United States when we leave, and I was wondering —do Rápidex employees drive the trucks, or do you have trucks that customers can rent?"

"All of our trucks are driven by drivers who are

fully trained in moving art with the greatest care," the woman replied proudly. "We do not rent out the trucks."

"Hmm," Nancy said, her mind racing. Then someone from Rápidex *had* to be involved in the smuggling.

"How large are the pieces you would like to move?" the saleswoman asked. "We have trucks available in many different sizes."

"It's hard to describe," Nancy said vaguely. "Do you think my friend here could see the trucks herself?" She shot Claire a meaningful glance, then shot one at the computer station. She hoped Claire would get the message: to distract the woman so Nancy could check out the computer records.

"Yes! I really would like to see the trucks myself," Claire jumped in, giving Nancy a secret wink. "You know, we artists are very temperamental when it comes to our work. I need to be sure that the truck will be the right one before I can make arrangements."

"I'll stay here," Nancy offered. "If any other customers come, I'll let you know right away."

The woman hesitated for a moment before answering. "Well, all right. The trucks are this way."

The woman led Claire behind the counter and through the open doorway. As soon as they were gone, Nancy hurried behind the counter and closed the door all but a crack. She knew she had to work quickly. Any second anyone could come in.

Going over to the computer, she scanned the computer's menu, then used the mouse to highlight what she hoped was the company's shipping records. The next thing Nancy knew, a list blinked onto the computer screen. Different columns showed customers' names, as well as where and when the trucks were sent.

Great! This looks like a chronological list of all the people who've rented Rápidex trucks, Nancy thought, skimming down the entries. She didn't see Maria Sandoval's name, but one particular listing caught her eye.

"Sam Breslin," she murmured. The sculptor had made arrangements to rent a truck just the day before. It was to be delivered to him in San Miguel the following Tuesday.

Nancy quickly scrolled back through the entries for the previous few months. "What do you know," she said under her breath.

Since January, Sam Breslin had rented half a dozen trucks. Each time, his destination was Los Angeles. If someone from the institute was helping Mexicans cross the border to the U.S. illegally, Sam Breslin had just become a likely candidate.

"I think that last truck you showed me will be just right."

Claire's voice broke into Nancy's thoughts, and she realized with a start that Claire and the other woman were coming back to the sales office! Nancy ran back around to the other side of the counter. Before she could reach over and clear the computer screen, however, the woman came through the doorway.

"Shall I make the reservation for you now?" the woman inquired pleasantly, while Claire circled around the counter to rejoin Nancy.

73

"That won't be necessary," Nancy said quickly, but the saleswoman had already stepped over to the computer station.

Nancy held her breath when she saw the puzzled expression on the saleswoman's face. "This should not be here," the woman murmured. For a brief instant her eyes fell on Nancy. Then she shrugged and threw her hands in the air. "I will never understand this computer."

Nancy laughed nervously, then turned to Claire with a meaningful look. "We'd better get going."

"I guess we'll hold off making the reservations until we know, uh, the exact date we'll need the truck," Claire added. After thanking the saleswoman, the two girls left the Rápidex office.

"You found out something, didn't you?" Claire asked once they were outside.

Nancy told Claire about the trucks Sam Breslin had rented over the past few months. "He just arranged for another truck, too, for next Tuesday."

"So you think *he's* the one who's smuggling illegal aliens in the trucks?" Claire asked.

"I can't be sure," Nancy replied. "But if he is, he's probably working with someone from Rápidex, since he can't drive the truck on his own."

Claire was thoughtful. "You know, he might really be using the trucks to ship artwork, but six truckloads sound like a lot more than anyone usually sends back to the States in six months."

"We'll have to try to find out more about that when we get back to San Miguel," Nancy said. "Did you see anything unusual in the garage?"

Claire shrugged. "Just a bunch of trucks," she

replied. "Oh—there *was* something else, but I don't know if it's important. There's another office connected to the loading dock. I saw a guy come out of it while the woman was showing me trucks."

"Another office?" Nancy glanced quickly back at the Rápidex building. "I'd love to get a look in there, but how can we . . ."

Her voice trailed off as a bright blue truck pulled into a narrow drive right next to her and Claire. The drive led to the back of the Rápidex building and opened onto what looked like a parking lot.

"I know exactly how!" she said. "Come on!"

She gestured for Claire to follow her down the drive. At the end of the drive she paused to survey the scene. A few trucks were parked in the lot. The truck they had seen was just pulling through an open doorway into the garage.

"Great! That's the outside entrance," Nancy said. "All we have to do is make our way through there and into that office without anyone seeing us."

"You mean, sneak in?" Claire asked with concern. "Are you sure that's a good idea?"

"It's the only way I can think of to check out the office," Nancy said. "I can go alone if—"

"I'm coming, too," Claire said resolutely. She took a deep breath, then let it out slowly. "Okay, let's do it."

The two girls hurried over to the garage door, then stopped just outside. Peeking her head around, Nancy saw rows of parked trucks. A man was just getting out of one, and Nancy watched as he walked to a door on the opposite side of the garage and went through it. Otherwise, the garage seemed empty.

Nancy gave a go-ahead nod to Claire, then stepped quietly inside. "Where was the office you saw?" she whispered.

Claire nodded to the right, and Nancy saw a closed door about twenty-five feet away. Keeping close to the trucks, the two girls quickly made their way to the door. Nancy pressed her ear against it, and when she didn't hear anything, she tried the knob.

"Good, it's open," she whispered to Claire. A moment later they were inside with the door closed behind them.

The small room was stiflingly hot, despite two small windows set high in the outside wall. Nancy immediately felt beads of sweat form at her hairline, but she didn't dare turn about the small fan resting on the desk. Some blue Rápidex uniforms hung on hooks on the wall. Next to them were two rickety chairs and a low table with empty soda bottles and an ashtray overflowing with cigarette butts. Grimy rags and tools were scattered about the rusty metal shelves, and smudges of oil stained the metal desk.

"I'm almost afraid to touch anything," Claire whispered, crinkling up her nose. "Let's get out of here. I doubt we'll find anything in all this junk."

Nancy was already circling the room. "This looks like some sort of lounge for the truck drivers," she said. "If one of the drivers is involved, there could be evidence here."

She decided to start with the desk. The scarred

desktop was empty except for a container of cold coffee, so she pulled out the only drawer.

"String, packing tape, pens . . ." Nancy rummaged around. "Nothing here that shouldn't be," she said, disappointed.

Claire bent over the drawer, her brow furrowed. "Doesn't this drawer look a little shallow?"

"You're right!" Nancy said. "The outside of the drawer is about six inches deep, but the inside depth can't be more than three or four inches."

Nancy felt a rush of excitement as she pulled out the drawer and dumped its contents on top of the desk. Then she tugged at the metal bottom until she was able to wrench it free.

"I don't believe it," Claire whispered in amazement. "There *is* a compartment!"

There was only one item in the secret compartment, a worn spiral notebook. Nancy hurriedly pulled it out and opened it—then gave a low whistle as she gazed at the columns of dates and notations.

"Camiones . . . número de viajeros . . . coyotes," she murmured, reading the headings.

"Coyotes? That's the name used for people who ferry foreigners across the border!" Claire cut in.

"Claire, we hit the jackpot," Nancy whispered. "This looks like records of the trucks and drivers who took people across the border."

She gazed down the list, but it was hard to make sense of the notations. Most were just initials. "JPF, EC, RM, EC . . ." Nancy murmured. She didn't see the initials SB or anything else that might show that Sam Breslin was involved.

"I don't know who *EC* is, but he's on this list more than any other coyote," Nancy whispered. "Claire, can you think of—"

"Nancy!" Claire's harsh whisper made Nancy stop short. Claire was by the door, and she was terrified. "Someone's coming!"

Nancy jumped into action, slamming the notebook closed and shoving it back in the drawer. A second later, she had refitted the false bottom and was frantically shoving back all the contents she had dumped on the desktop. She had just closed the drawer when the door swung open.

At first, all Nancy saw was a squat, thick silhouette. Then, as the person stepped inside, Nancy got a better look at his broad features and crooked, flattened nose.

Nancy's breath caught in her throat. He was the man she and Joe had seen in Benito Juárez Park!

Chapter

Nine

NANCY'S BLOOD WENT COLD. When the man's gaze fell on her and Claire, he stopped short.

Please don't recognize me, Nancy silently begged. Then she remembered that it would have been almost impossible for him to have gotten a good look at her in the park.

"Qué hacen aquí?" the man finally said.

Nancy tried to stifle the bubble of fear in her throat. Next to her Claire had backed up against the desk. She was gripping it so tightly that her knuckles were white. Giving the man what she hoped was a convincing smile, Nancy fibbed, "I'm sorry, but we don't speak Spanish—"

She flashed Claire a look that said "play along," then gave a helpless wave of her hands. "I'm afraid we're totally lost. We need the nearest metro stop, and somehow we ended up here. I was hoping to find a map or something to help us—"

"That's right. A map." Claire stepped forward, swallowing hard. "We're, uh, terrible with directions," she added. "Can you please tell us how to get to the Zócalo?"

"Is not the tourist office," he growled. "Is a private business. What are you doing in this area?"

Think fast, Drew! Nancy ordered herself. "We, uh, wanted to get a look at the *real* Mexico—you know, the part of the city that isn't for visitors," she said.

"Mexico City's underbelly is really fascinating," Claire put in with an innocent look. "Not at all like San Miguel de Allende—"

"What do you know about San Miguel de Allende?" the burly man asked suspiciously.

"N-nothing!" Claire answered in a high-pitched voice.

"We were just visiting there, that's all," Nancy added quickly. San Miguel was obviously a topic to avoid around this guy. "About the Zócalo," she said, trying to change the subject. "Do you think you could help us, Mr.—?"

If she could get the man to reveal his name, they might be able to find out if his initials corresponded to any of those she'd seen in the book.

"Enough!" the man burst out. His face was tight as he took another step into the office. "You must leave—immediately!"

"Sure. Sorry to bother you, sir," Nancy said quickly. Grabbing Claire by the arm, she pulled her around the burly man and out of the office. "Thanks for all your help. 'Bye, now."

As the two girls hurried away, Nancy could feel the man's gaze on her. She didn't start to breathe easily until they had reached the street, hailed a taxi, and were safely inside.

After giving the driver their address, Claire sank back against the taxi seat. "Phew!" she exclaimed. "That guy was scary! I bet anything he's mixed up in this smuggling business."

"Me, too," Nancy agreed. "This isn't the first time I've seen him, either. That's the guy Joe and I saw in the park last night."

"The one who tried to run Joe down?" Claire asked, her green eyes widening. "Do you think he recognized you?"

Nancy was thoughtful as she stared out the taxi window. "I'm not sure, but he definitely reacted when you mentioned San Miguel."

"I'll say!" Claire exclaimed. "I practically died when—"

She suddenly broke off and stared out her window. "Hey, isn't that the guy from the gallery—the one Mr. Perelis punched?"

"Quentin Cole?" Nancy leaned forward to follow Claire's gaze. The tall art collector was sauntering through the wrought-iron gate to a hotel. "It *is* him. Maybe that's where he's staying."

Nancy squinted, trying to read the sign above the gate. "Villa Flores," she murmured.

"I bet Frank and Joe will appreciate learning where their top suspect's hotel is," Claire said. "We can tell them at dinner."

Nancy smiled. "Good idea, although I wouldn't be surprised if they already know where he's staying. Frank and Rosa did follow Cole. Who knows? Maybe they've already solved their case."

"I can't believe we're back at square one," Joe said grumpily. "Our top suspect got away. For all we know, he's escaped with the jade mask for good."

He leaned against the edge of a stone fountain and watched people circulating around Alameda Park. When Frank and Rosa had returned to the Galería Perelis, the opening was winding down. Bess had left for the girls' hotel to meet Claire and Nancy before dinner, while Ricardo stayed behind with his father to call collectors who had lent masks for the exhibit and reassure them that their works of art would be safe. Frank, Joe, and Rosa had decided to get out of the way while the cleanup crew went to work, so they had gone to the park.

"What can I say? Rosa and I were struck by an irresistible urge to drop in on a wedding—literally," Frank said. "I can't believe the bride and groom didn't even invite us to their reception."

Despite Frank's joke, Joe didn't miss the tight set of his brother's jaw or the narrowing of his eyes. Frank was obviously more bothered about losing Cole than he was letting on.

"Don't sweat it," Joe said. He turned his head, following the progress of a group of girls walking arm in arm, talking.

"This park is a very popular meeting place,"

Rosa spoke up from her seat on a bench near the fountain. "It's beautiful, but also treacherous. Many people were burned to death here during the Inquisition in the fifteen and sixteen hundreds."

Talk about beautiful but treacherous, Joe thought, shooting Rosa a hooded glance. Rosa had made it pretty obvious that she hated her father for banning Jim Stanton from her life. The question was, how far would she go to get back at him?

"Sounds delightful," Frank cracked.

"You are both too serious for me," she said, standing up. "I am going to go back to our apartment to take a shower before dinner. I need one after trying to get my moped to a mechanic."

"Sorry it was totaled," Frank said. "Joe and I will stop back at your dad's gallery to make sure everything's okay. Then we'll pick you up for dinner."

Rosa nodded, then walked away. Now that she was gone, Joe was finally able to ask the question that had been on his mind.

"Frank, are you sure it was an accident that Cole got away?" he asked. "I mean, Rosa was driving. So far she actually seems amused by all the trouble the stolen mask has caused. Maybe she thought it would be fun to botch our investigation, too."

"She didn't do it on purpose, I'm almost positive," he said in a voice that warned Joe to drop the subject. "What happened at the gallery after Rosa and I left?"

"Not much. When Mr. Perelis bashed Cole in the nose, it kind of put a damper on things," Joe said.

"Well, we've still got leads to follow," Frank said. "We should question the night guard. And we need to track down the stamped tin ornament—"

"Mr. Perelis and the police already talked to the night guard," Joe cut in. "Gerardo something or another. The guy said he was picked up by a friend right after Ramirez let him out of the gallery, and the police told Mr. Perelis that his story checked out."

Frank frowned. "So it seems we can count him out. Still, Cole—or *whoever* stole the mask—had to be working with someone. One person couldn't have handled that glass case alone."

"Which brings us to Juan Ramirez," Joe said. He pushed away from the fountain, stepped over to the bench, and sat down. "Now, there's a guy I *really* don't trust. He asked a lot of questions about where you and Rosa went. And even after the gallery emptied out and the night guard showed up, he still wanted to stick around. He only left because Mr. P. insisted on it."

"We're going to have to tell Mr. Perelis what we think," Frank said. "Considering how much he trusts Ramirez, it's not going to be easy." Glancing at his watch, he added, "We've been here for almost an hour. They should have finished cleaning up the gallery by now. Let's head back."

As the Hardys left the park, Joe suddenly stopped. "Oh—I almost forgot to mention that I made some phone calls about the hand ornament."

"You?" Frank paused on the sidewalk and shot him a look of open disbelief. "Joe, you can't even order a cup of coffee in Spanish."

"Okay, so maybe Mr. Perelis did the actual speaking, but I was right there," Joe said, grinning. "The point is, we found out something interesting. That particular ornament is only made by one company—Bombillas."

"Yeah?" A spark of interest lit up Frank's eyes. "So maybe we can track down our thief through that company," he said. "It's a long shot, but I don't think we can afford to overlook it."

The Hardys reached the gallery just as the two cleaning women were leaving. The guard, a big man with curly hair and dark skin, didn't look as if he was going to let them in, until Mr. Perelis appeared at the door.

"It's okay, Gerardo. These two are guests of mine, Frank and Joe Hardy," Mr. Perelis explained. He ushered the boys into the reception area.

The guard locked the door behind Frank and Joe. After activating the alarm, he stood next to the door, crossed his arms over his chest, and stared stonily at the Hardys.

"Um, could Frank and I talk to you privately for a moment, Mr. Perelis?" Joe asked.

Mr. Perelis glanced at Gerardo, then nodded. "We can talk in my office, in the back." He started through the doorway to the main gallery, then stopped when the phone on the reception desk rang.

"I hope this isn't another reporter," he said. With a weary sigh, he stepped back to the reception desk and picked up the receiver. *"Hola."* He listened, then said, "One moment," and held out the phone to Frank and Joe. "It is for you."

Joe grabbed the phone. "Hello?" No one answered, so he said again, "Hello? Is anybody there?"

Finally Joe heard a noise, and then a muffled man's voice spoke over the line: "Back off the case—if you want to live to make your flight back to the United States."

Chapter

Ten

WHO IS THIS?" Joe said into the phone, but his only answer was a dial tone.

"Trouble?" Frank guessed.

Joe nodded as he dropped the receiver back in its cradle. "Some bozo just tried to warn us off the case," he said.

"This is terrible," Mr. Perelis said. "Three collectors have threatened to pull their masks from my show if the jade mask is not recovered quickly. And now this—" He briefly closed his eyes and rubbed his temples with his fingertips. Then he looked at Frank and Joe. "I am grateful for all you've done so far, but I cannot risk you two being hurt."

"We'll be fine," Frank insisted. "There's no way we're going to let one phone call stop us. Joe, did you recognize the voice?"

"I know it was a guy, but I couldn't make out any special accent," Joe answered. "He sounded like he was speaking through a handkerchief."

"The person spoke English to me, but he may have had an accent. Since I am not a native speaker, it is not easy for me to tell," Mr. Perelis added. "I do not understand. I have told no one you are investigating this case, but the person asked for you by name."

"Quentin Cole?" Frank suggested. "He did see me following him before."

Judging by the meaningful look Frank shot him, Joe knew he was thinking of another suspect, too—Juan Ramirez. He decided against mentioning the guard. Seeing Mr. Perelis's tired face and stooped posture, Joe decided that the gallery owner had had enough bad news for one day. But he didn't know how much longer he and Frank could put off talking to Mr. Perelis.

"Here we are," Claire announced. She came to a halt on the Calle Florencia and turned to Nancy and Bess. "Café Quetzalcoatl."

"Already?" Bess glanced around the street, which was closed to traffic. Tourists bustled around on their way to and from the many open-air restaurants. "I was having so much fun walking around the Zona Rosa that I'm almost sorry to stop."

"It's a fun neighborhood, but I *am* getting kind of hungry," Nancy said. "It's after nine."

She saw that the group of tables they had stopped in front of were nestled beneath arching wrought-iron trellises draped with roses. A man wearing a colorful serape wove among the tables, playing a guitar and singing. At the rear of the restaurant, she could just make out Frank's dark hair.

"Frank and Joe are already here," she said, pointing.

"And Ricardo," Bess added, waving. "Hi, you guys!" she called.

"So what's going on between you and Ricardo?" Claire asked, raising an eyebrow at Bess.

Bess's cheeks turned pink. "Well, we're not going to get married or anything if that's what you mean. I can't imagine having a long-term relationship with a guy who lives in another country. But we've been having a really nice time. Ricardo's a great guy."

Nancy smiled as they made their way to the table. Somehow, Bess always managed to find just the right amount of romance wherever she went.

"I see you found the place," Joe said, holding aside a rose branch that was in the way. "Ouch! Ricardo and Rosa say the food is great here, but I don't know—this decor is deadly."

Claire grinned at Joe as she stepped carefully around the rose bush and sat down. "I'm sure a couple of crack detectives like you and Frank can handle it."

Frank winced. "A crack detective is exactly what I *wasn't* today," he said, clenching his jaw.

"Things didn't go well when you followed Quentin Cole?" Nancy guessed.

"It was a total bust," Frank said. "Cole got away."

"No thanks to the local help," Joe muttered.

Judging by the way he was glaring at Rosa, Nancy had a pretty good idea to whom he was referring.

Rosa glowered back at him. "We are not all so interested in your little investigation," she said hotly. "Some of us have lives of our own, you know."

Nancy exchanged uncomfortable glances with Bess and Claire. Something was definitely going on. The tension at the table was unbelievable.

"Let's just forget about it, okay?" Frank said, giving Joe a warning look. Then he picked up a menu. "So, what does everyone want to order?"

"Quetzalcoatl is the name of one of the most important Aztec gods," Ricardo explained. "The specialties here are all traditional Aztec dishes from the days before Spanish colonization." Nancy thought he seemed relieved to change the subject. "There is pheasant or quail, if you like."

"What are *chapulines?*" Bess asked, raising her eyes from her menu.

Ricardo gave her a mischievous smile. "Grasshoppers," he answered. "They are almost as delicious as the *escamoles*—ants' eggs."

"Ugh!" Bess's mouth dropped open in horror. "Thanks, but I think I'll stick with the quail."

"I'll have the *tacos de huitlacoche,*" Claire said. "They're made from a special kind of corn."

Nancy decided to try the pheasant. While the others were deciding, she told the Hardys about seeing Quentin Cole, then gave them the name of the hotel and the address. "It's near here, actually."

"Thanks for the tip. After what happened earlier

this evening, we could use it," Frank said. "What about *your* case? Any luck at Rápidex?"

Keeping her voice low, Nancy told the Hardys about the record book and about the encounter with the man who had tried to run Joe down.

"Sounds like that guy might be one of the drivers who's ferrying Mexicans across the border," Joe said, leaning forward in his chair.

"Probably," Nancy agreed. "But it's too risky to go back to Rápidex. If he sees us again, I doubt he'll let us off so easy. Claire, Bess, and I decided we'll be better off going back to San Miguel tomorrow to follow our other new lead."

Frank nodded. "That sculptor, Breslin."

"Maybe through him you'll be able to learn more about that truck driver," Ricardo put in.

Nancy hadn't realized that the others were listening, too. "You guys, it's important to keep this quiet," she said. "Any leak could screw up our investigation."

Joe nodded toward Rosa and mumbled, "Someone here already knows a lot about screwing up an investigation."

"Cool it, Joe," Frank said sharply.

Rosa's face turned bright red. "I don't have to put up with this!" she burst out, her amber eyes flashing. "You are nothing but an arrogant jerk!"

"At least I'm not trying to wreck my own father's career!" Joe shot back.

"You don't know anything about my father and me. Why don't you just stay away from me!" Rosa jumped to her feet, knocking her chair to the ground. With a final scathing look at Joe, she stormed from the restaurant.

For a moment everyone just stared at one another. Then Frank said, "Good going, brother. You just alienated our host."

"She deserved it," Joe grumbled.

"You are wrong about Rosa, Joe," Ricardo said forcefully. "She is rebellious, but she would never do anything to harm our father. I wish you would stop being so mean to her."

Joe took a deep breath, then let it out slowly. "I'm sorry," he told Ricardo. "I'll try to be nice to her from now on."

Ricardo nodded, but Nancy could tell that he was still upset. He hardly said a word while they ate. As soon as the waiter took away their plates, Ricardo got to his feet and put some bills on the table. "I'm sorry to leave early, but I want to see how Rosa is." He turned to the Hardys. "I hope you will not think it rude of me to leave. I will see you back at the house later."

"That's fine," Frank said. "We'll make sure the girls get back to their hotel."

Looking apologetically at Bess, Ricardo asked, "Do you mind?"

"Of course not," Bess assured him with a smile. "Will you still be able to go to that outdoor crafts market with us tomorrow morning?"

"The Bazar Sábado," Ricardo said. "Of course. I will meet you at your hotel in the morning. *Buenas noches,* everyone."

After Ricardo left, Frank turned to his brother. "Listen, Joe, it's not a great idea to—"

"I know, I know. I should have kept my suspicions about Rosa private," Joe said. "From now on I promise to be a model of tact."

After they had paid their bill, Claire checked her watch and said, "It's after eleven. Maybe it's time for the rest of us to call it a night, too."

One look at Joe, and Frank knew his brother was thinking the same thing he was. "We'll take you back to your hotel," Frank told the girls. "Then Joe and I are going to make a stop at the Villa de Flores."

"Need any help?" Nancy asked, her blue eyes alive with interest. "I'm not ready to go back to the hotel."

"I'm game, too," Claire agreed. "After today, I'm getting used to this cloak-and-dagger stuff."

Bess grinned. "Count me in," she said. "I'm not about to miss out on any more investigating than I already have!"

Calle Londres was the first cross street they came to when they walked south from the restaurant. "I think the hotel is this way," Nancy said, turning east. After a few blocks, she stopped in front of the wrought-iron gate of the Villa Flores. "This is the place, guys," she announced.

"What's the plan of action?" Bess asked Frank and Joe.

Frank peeked through the hotel's entrance. It opened onto a courtyard dotted with tables, potted plants, and flowers. Rooms stretched around the courtyard on two floors. All along the second floor was a balcony of ornate metal railings and plaster pilasters. A man and woman were sitting at one of the tables talking, but otherwise the hotel was quiet.

"The first thing to do is find out which room is Quentin Cole's," Frank said. He took another peek through the entrance. "I think I see a reception area over there, to the left."

"Say no more." Joe held up a hand. "I'll find out the room number from the receptionist, then distract her with my amazing charm while you guys check out Cole's room."

"What if the receptionist is a man?" Claire asked.

Joe was lost in thought for a moment, then snapped his fingers. "Bess, come with me."

"Good enough," Nancy agreed, laughing. "Between the two of you, you could charm any girl *or* guy."

After the way their case had gone so far, Frank wasn't in the mood to joke around. "Be sure to say the room number loud enough for us to hear," he told Joe and Bess. "Then Nancy and I will go up to Cole's room. If he's not there, we'll search it. If he is, we'll have to think of a way to get him out of the room." He turned to Claire. "You keep watch here. If Cole isn't in his room and he suddenly shows up, whistle loudly twice."

Claire nodded. "Sure thing."

Leaving her outside the gate, Frank and Nancy stepped inside and crouched in the shadow of an azalea bush just off the courtyard. From there, Frank had a good view of the open wooden door to the left and the reception area beyond.

"Buenos nachos, señorita."

Frank groaned when he heard his brother's botched Spanish greeting. Next to him, Nancy chuckled softly. "It sounds as if he's greeting the menu at a taco stand!" she whispered.

Frank and Nancy listened while Joe explained to the receptionist that he and his girlfriend wanted to visit Mr. Quentin Cole.

"What was that you said?" Joe was saying. "He's in room *twenty-four,* on the balcony?"

Frank caught Nancy's quick nod—she had heard the room number, too. He held up a hand gesturing for her to wait until they were sure Joe and Bess had distracted the receptionist.

Suddenly Bess's outraged voice rang into the courtyard. "Don't deny it. You were flirting with the receptionist just now. How could you!"

"Honey, I was not," Joe said soothingly. Frank could just imagine his phony expression. "Please, don't cry, sweetheart. Miss, could you please show my girlfriend to the ladies' room?"

Frank could hear the woman start to object, but Joe cut in. "Please," he said forcefully.

A moment later Frank could see the receptionist leading Bess to a room off the reception area. Turning to Nancy, he grinned and gave her the thumbs-up sign.

"Let's rock 'n' roll," he whispered.

The two of them silently entered the courtyard, then paused to take stock of the situation. A metal stairway rose up to the balcony from the courtyard. Large potted ferns dotted the upper balcony, but

Nancy could still make out the small lights next to each door that illuminated the room's number.

"Up there," Nancy whispered, pointing to the second doorway to the right of the stairway.

Frank squinted and was able to make out the blue ceramic tile with a glazed white *24* on it. He was glad to see that the couple in the courtyard had left. A quick glance at the reception area told him that the receptionist and Bess hadn't returned yet. The coast was clear.

Nancy was a step ahead of him as they slipped around the edge of the courtyard. Suddenly a scraping noise from somewhere above caught Frank's attention, and he looked up. "What?"

A huge ceramic planter with a fern was resting precariously on the thin iron rail next to one of the pilasters. There was no way it could balance there by itself. Someone had to be holding it, but from this angle, Frank couldn't see who it was.

"What is it, Frank?"

Frank's gaze moved to Nancy, and he realized with a jolt that she was standing right underneath the planter!

"Nan, look out!" he shouted. Before the words were out of his mouth, the ceramic planter teetered over the edge and plummeted—right toward Nancy's head!

Chapter

Eleven

NANCY FROZE when she saw the panic on Frank's face. "What's going—"

"*Ooomph!*"

She felt the wind being knocked out of her as Frank catapulted into her, throwing her to one side. They hit the paving stones hard, tumbling over in a tangle of arms and legs.

A split second later there was a deafening crash right next to them. Dirt and cracked bits of clay showered over her and Frank. Nancy saw a broken, uprooted fern resting in what was left of its planter. Next to her, Frank was standing up, brushing dirt from his arms and legs.

"Are you all right?" he asked Nancy, his eyes filled with concern. He reached out for her hand and helped her to her feet.

Nancy nodded as she tried to catch her breath. "Thanks, Frank," she finally managed to say. "If it weren't for you, I'd probably be wearing that planter as a hat right now."

Bess and Joe, followed by the receptionist, ran into the courtyard from the reception area.

"What happened!" Bess exclaimed. "Are you okay?"

Frank gazed grimly up at the second-floor balcony. "I think someone threw—"

"Good evening!"

The jovial voice came from above them, and Nancy saw Quentin Cole jogging easily down the circular staircase from the balcony. He was now wearing crisp chinos, a white button-down shirt, and shiny brown leather loafers. Nancy couldn't help noticing that he looked like an advertisement for expensive men's clothing.

"Is gardening a hobby of yours?" Quentin Cole asked, pausing at the foot of the stairs to look at the broken planter. "Though this seems an unlikely spot to be digging up dirt, I must say."

Joe clenched his hands into fists at his sides. "This *gardening* stint, as you call it, wasn't exactly voluntary, pal. Someone threw this planter over the wall at my friends."

The receptionist gasped and mumbled something about *la policía.*

"There's no need to call the authorities," Cole said smoothly. He seemed completely unruffled. Nancy thought she even detected a glint of amusement in his eyes. "No one was hurt, and I didn't see a soul up there. It must have been the wind."

"Yeah, right. You mean a *windbag* named Quentin Cole," Frank muttered.

Cole's easy smile didn't break for a moment. "Life is too short to waste it in anger and suspicion," he said to Frank. "I advise strongly against it. It isn't good for your health—if you know what I mean." He gave a breezy wave, then said, "We'll have to chat again sometime, but now I must be off."

Nancy shook her head as she watched Quentin Cole disappear through the hotel's wrought-iron gate. She turned back to her friends. "Am I crazy, or was that a threat?"

"It was a threat, all right," Joe said. "But by prancing out of here like that, he left us a golden opportunity." He glanced up at Quentin Cole's room, then nodded toward the receptionist, who had gotten a broom and dustpan and was starting to clean up the mess from the broken planter.

Joe jumped forward, taking the broom from the young woman. "Here, miss, my girlfriend and I can take care of that," he offered. "Just show us where we can get another broom."

While Bess and Joe went back into the office with the receptionist, Nancy flew up the stairs behind Frank to room 24. It took only a few seconds for Frank to pop the lock with a credit card.

After closing the wooden blinds, Frank flicked on the lights. Apart from a bed, night table, and small chest of drawers, there was just a luggage rack with Cole's open suitcase on it.

"You take the chest of drawers and the night table, while I check in here," Frank said, moving toward Cole's open suitcase. "Look for any sign of the mask, or for a tin ornament shaped like a hand."

"The thief's calling card," Nancy remembered, striding over to the chest of drawers. A thorough search didn't turn up anything, so she turned to the bedside table. On it a phone directory lay open.

"Hey, look at this, Frank," she said. "It's open to the *R*'s. I wonder what Cole was looking up?"

As Frank came to stand next to her, he asked, "Hey, is there a Ramirez on that page?"

"Over a dozen of them," Nancy answered. "Wait a second! Someone underlined one of them: 'Ramirez, Juan,'" she read, then looked up at Frank. "Mr. Perelis's guard. Why would Quentin Cole want his phone number or address?"

"Maybe they're working together," Frank suggested. Then he corrected himself. "No, that doesn't make sense. If they were working together, Cole wouldn't need to look up his number."

A noise from the courtyard below caught Nancy's attention. "Let's finish looking around. We can talk about this later—after we're safely out of here."

She was just finishing checking under the bed when Frank emerged from the closet. "Nothing," he said in disgust. "I should have known that Cole wouldn't leave a priceless jade mask lying around."

"Especially since he didn't seem to mind leaving the hotel with us still here," Nancy pointed out. She got to her feet and brushed her hands together.

Frank raked a hand back through his wavy, dark brown hair. "I guess Joe and I can't put it off any longer. We have to talk to Mr. Perelis about Juan Ramirez."

"You boys are wrong about Juan," Mr. Perelis told Frank and Joe the next morning. He frowned as he stirred his coffee. "He has been working at my gallery for over ten years. We have sometimes argued about salary, yes, but he would never betray me."

Joe rubbed his eyes and looked at his brother across the Perelises' modern glass dining room table. Despite the fact that they'd gotten home after two in the morning, he and Frank had forced themselves out of bed when they heard Mr. Perelis in the dining room. As Joe had suspected, the gallery owner had been anything but happy to hear their suspicions of his guard.

"If he's innocent, then why does he keep giving Joe and me such a hard time?" Frank asked.

Joe leaned forward. "And why was Quentin Cole looking up his number?"

Mr. Perelis shook his head wearily. "There could be many reasons that have nothing to do with the jade mask," he insisted. "The police have already questioned him, and they do not think he is involved. That is enough for me."

Frank shot Joe an uneasy look, then said to Mr. Perelis, "I know this is hard for you, but we have to check out every lead. If—"

"I trust Juan completely," Mr. Perelis cut in. He glanced at his watch, then stood up suddenly. "Come. I will prove it to you."

Joe and Frank followed Mr. Perelis to the front door. "Where are we going?" Joe asked.

"To the gallery," Mr. Perelis replied. "After last night's opening, I was finally able to convince Juan to take today off. I do not approve of your going through his personal things there, but if it will convince you that he had nothing to do with stealing the jade mask . . ."

"Thanks, Mr. Perelis," Frank said.

They arrived at the gallery before nine. Juan's replacement was there. After asking the guard to keep watch at the front door, Mr. Perelis led Frank and Joe through a door at the rear of the gallery.

"This part of the gallery is not open to the public," Mr. Perelis said. "My office is there," he said, pointing to a closed door at the end of a small hallway. "Here are the guards' lockers."

Mr. Perelis had paused next to a recessed area in the hallway. Four lockers were set into it, Joe saw, each with a combination lock. "This one is Juan's," Mr. Perelis added, tapping a locker. "I have the combination in my office."

"Great," Joe said when Mr. Perelis opened the locker door a few moments later. The brothers closed in on the locker at the same time and began sifting through its contents.

"Doesn't look like much," Frank said, checking the garments hanging from a metal hook. "A uniform, T-shirt—nothing in the pockets."

Joe felt around the locker bottom. "Not much here, either. Just some cigarettes and matches," he said, picking them up.

"See?" Mr. Perelis said, relieved. "I hope now you will leave Juan alone."

"Mmm," Joe flipped the matches over in his hands absentmindedly. "I was *sure* we'd find something, but—"

"Hey, what's that?" Frank cut him off.

Joe held up the matches. "These? There's nothing here to . . ." His voice trailed off as he spotted the inked notation on the matchbook cover. "Looks like our friend Ramirez wrote something down: '4753 La Gama Drive, Los Angeles, California,'" he read. He looked over at Frank and shrugged. "Maybe the guy met someone who lives in L.A. So?"

"So, Los Angeles only happens to be one of the biggest art centers in the country, *and* it's the closest major U.S. city to Japan," Frank said.

"You're right!" Joe exclaimed. "If Ramirez and his accomplice"—he shot a quick look at Mr. Perelis—"or whoever the thieves are, wanted to sell the jade mask or ship it to a wealthy buyer in Japan, Los Angeles would be a good place for them to take it."

He showed the matchbook to Mr. Perelis. "Is this Juan Ramirez's handwriting?"

The gallery owner nodded. "Many people from Los Angeles have been to my gallery," he said defensively. "That doesn't mean . . .

"I still think Juan is innocent, but I will do what I can to find out where this address is," he assured the Hardys.

"Thanks," Frank said. He wrote down the address for Mr. Perelis, then glanced at his watch. "We'd better get a move on, Joe. We're supposed to meet Nancy and everyone at the Bazar Sábado at ten."

"The whole city must have decided to show up here," Frank said an hour later, after being jostled to the side by a Mexican woman with three small children in tow.

"I can't believe we didn't arrange a specific meeting place to hook up with everyone," Joe said.

Shading his eyes from the strong sunlight, Frank glanced around the bustling bazaar. He and Joe had only made it halfway down one row so far, but they had already seen silver jewelry and belt buckles, handwoven blankets, ceramic tiles, and a display of papier-mâché masks. Some vendors had rigged up overhead tarps to protect their tables from the sun, while others simply displayed their crafts on blankets on the ground. The air was filled with the smells of sweets and fried food, and with the loud exclamations of people bargaining.

"I guess we should just keep moving," said Frank. "We'll find them eventually."

They had just passed a stand of brightly painted carved wooden fish, when Joe nodded ahead. "Check out the entertainment."

A group of musicians were playing guitars and flutes at the end of the row of crafts stands. People had crowded around to watch them.

"We can look at all this stuff later, Joe. First we've got to find the girls and Ricardo," Frank said firmly, scanning the crowd.

He pushed his way around a woman heatedly arguing with a blanket vendor. Coming toward them was a muscular man dressed in crisp black pants that flared below the knees. His white shirt was tucked into a multicolored striped cloth wrapped around his waist, and he also wore a short black bolero jacket that flared into bells below his elbows. A half mask added to his dramatic appearance.

"Check out the Lone Ranger," Joe said, laughing.

"I think he's a mariachi dancer," Frank said. "From what I've heard, it's really popular here."

Suddenly Joe's expression turned serious. "Maybe the guy didn't like that crack I made," he said in a low voice. "He's coming over here, and he doesn't seem too happy."

Frank saw that the masked dancer was only about six feet in front of them now. Through the mask's small holes, the man's eyes were chilling. This guy meant business.

"Hey, look," Frank began, "I'm sorry if my brother offended you, but—"

The mariachi dancer took another step toward him and Joe. He raised his hand, and sunlight glinted off something metallic. Frank's entire body tensed when he saw what it was.

"Joe, watch out!" he shouted. "He's got a knife!"

Chapter

Twelve

JOE HAD CAUGHT SIGHT OF the long knife blade just before Frank's warning. His heart racing, he reacted quickly.

Crouching low, he circled around to the mariachi dancer's left, so that he and Frank were on opposite sides of the man. "Hey! Didn't anyone ever tell you that it's not polite to carry lethal weapons in public?" he called out.

The mariachi dancer whirled around to face Joe. His mouth twisted into a snarl, and he jabbed his knife in Joe's direction.

"Come to papa," Joe said, jumping to his left. He knew that Frank was making his move.

A split second later the mariachi dancer's face twisted in pain as Frank's hands closed around his knife hand and squeezed hard.

"Aie!" the dancer cried, dropping the knife. Around them, a few people clapped and whistled. Apparently, they thought this was some kind of entertainment.

"Stay back!" Joe yelled, waving the spectators away. He turned to Frank just in time to see the mariachi dancer land a kick to Frank's chest that sent him flying backward. Then the guy knocked a teenage boy to one side and took off down a row of stands.

Joe was right behind him. "I'll meet you back here!" he called to Frank.

The mariachi dancer was barely visible in the crowd of people. Screams erupted as he crashed through a stand of copper items, sending pots and candlesticks clattering in all directions.

"Excuse us!" Joe called as he flew through the stand behind the mariachi dancer.

The masked man glanced briefly over his shoulder. When he saw Joe, he vaulted over some glazed ceramic plates and into the next row of stands.

Instead of jumping after the man, Joe kept running down the row of displays he was already in, his breath coming in ragged gasps that burned his throat. He raced through the crowd, knocking several shoppers down, but he ignored their outraged cries. His attention was focused on keeping the mariachi dancer in sight.

When Joe saw that the dancer was squarely to his left, on the other side of a display of woven blankets, he made his move. Using a pile of striped blankets as a jumping board, he vaulted through the display and landed in the aisle where the mariachi dancer was.

"What's your hurry?" Joe yelled as he caught hold of the man's flared black sleeve.

The dancer let out a cry of surprise and stumbled to his knees. All around them, people were scrambling and ducking. Joe tried to get a better hold of the mariachi dancer's arm, but the man flung him to the side with a surprisingly powerful thrust that sent Joe crashing through half a dozen papiermâché masks hanging from an awning.

"No!" Joe quickly regained his footing and took off after the man again. He gritted his teeth and poured on more speed. "You're mine, buddy—"

A moment later Joe smashed into a Japanese tourist who had just stepped in his way. The two of them fell in a heap on the ground. Joe tried to jump up, but his left arm was caught in the other man's camera strap. Finally he managed to tug his arm free and get up. He glanced wildly in every direction, but the mariachi dancer was nowhere to be seen.

"I don't believe it!" he cried, slamming his right fist into his left palm in frustration.

"Excuse me. You are all right?"

Joe saw the tourist gazing at him as the man brushed dirt from his clothes. "Uh, yeah. I'm fine," Joe said. "Sorry about running into you." Still breathing heavily, he turned and headed back to where he'd left Frank.

When he got there, Joe saw that Claire, Nancy, Bess, Rosa, and Ricardo were all with him.

"Well, at least Frank and I caught up with you guys," Joe said, forcing a smile. "Too bad I can't say the same about the guy I was just chasing."

"I'm just glad neither of you was hurt!" Claire exclaimed. "That man sounded dangerous."

"Frank told us what happened," Nancy added. "I wish we'd been around to help."

Frank rubbed his chest. "The guy got me right in the solar plexus. By the time I caught my breath, Joe, you and Mr. Mariachi were out of sight."

"Who do you think it was?" Ricardo asked.

"My guess is he's someone who doesn't want us investigating the theft of the mask," Joe said.

Rosa gave a nonchalant shrug. "Not everything that happens in the world is part of a mystery. Maybe he was just a crazy person who attacked you at random. It happens, you know."

Joe's gut instinct told him otherwise, but he decided not to mention that—not in front of Ricardo and Rosa, anyway. Still, he couldn't help wondering why Rosa kept belittling their investigation.

"It's too bad that lady who sells the costumes couldn't tell us anything," Bess added.

"Come again?" Joe asked, looking at Bess.

Bess pointed at the multicolored, striped woven belt she was wearing with her flowered shorts and T-shirt. "The woman who sells these also had mariachi costumes."

"The same kind that guy was wearing," Frank added.

"We told Frank about her as soon as we saw him

and heard about the attack," Nancy put in. "We questioned her, but—"

"She already sold a few today, but she couldn't remember what any of the buyers looked like," Frank explained.

"I don't get it. How could the person know you'd be here at the bazaar?" Claire asked Frank and Joe.

Joe was thoughtful for a moment, then said, "We did make the plans while we were at the gallery opening. Plenty of people were there," he pointed out. "The guy wasn't tall enough to be Quentin Cole, but he could have been Juan Ramirez."

Or Rosa could have tipped off the person, Joe added to himself.

"The muscular build was about right for Ramirez," Frank said. "And he had the day off."

Giving the Hardys a sympathetic look, Nancy said, "I wish we could help you two check him out, but we have to get back to San Miguel this afternoon to follow up on our own case."

"Besides, we have to be there for a dinner my mom and dad are giving for some of the institute's faculty," Claire added.

"I'll be returning with the girls," Ricardo said to Frank and Joe. "You do not mind?"

Actually, Joe was relieved to hear that Ricardo wouldn't be around. It would be easier to investigate without his being so defensive about his sister. "Don't worry about it," Joe said.

"Anyway, we're supposed to be having fun." Frank turned to the others and smiled. "Let's check this place out!"

* * *

"Mmm, those lemon trees smell heavenly," Bess said late that afternoon as she leaned back in her chair at the Instituto San Miguel's cantina.

Nancy nodded. "Mexico City is a great place to visit, but it's nice to be back in San Miguel."

"I'm glad we have a vacation home here," Ricardo commented. He turned to Bess and squeezed her hand. "Especially since I got to meet you."

Bess's face lit up with pleasure. "Let's order. After the drive back, I'm hungry."

Ricardo, Bess, Nancy, and Claire had gotten back to San Miguel by four o'clock. After dropping off their things at their houses, Claire had gone to the institute's sculpture studio to work on a project that was due. She had left the others at the cantina.

"I see we're not the only ones who are hungry," Nancy commented. "Isn't that Jim Stanton over there?" She nodded toward a table near the reflecting pool. Jim was bent over a book.

"Jim, hi!" Bess called out brightly with a wave.

When he looked up, Jim didn't seem to recognize them at first. Then he saw Ricardo and nodded to him. "Oh, right," he said to the two girls. "You're Rosa's friends." He took a sip of his coffee.

"Nancy and Bess," Nancy supplied. "Would you like to join us?"

Jim checked his watch, then stood up. He tucked his paperback into the back pocket of his jeans. "I'd like to, but I have to go."

"Time to get back to your studio?" Bess guessed. "Being a painter must be exciting."

Jim gave her a lazy look before answering. "Actually, right now I'm just meeting a friend," he said. "See you."

After leaving some coins on his table, he waved to them, then left the cantina.

"He's weird," Bess commented. "He's not exactly friendly *or* unfriendly."

"We haven't had much of a chance to get to know him," Nancy reminded Bess. Then, remembering why she and Bess were there, she gazed across the courtyard at the kitchen. "I don't see Maria Sandoval."

The rotund, dark-haired woman was nowhere to be seen. Instead, a girl who was about a year or two younger than Nancy slipped from behind the counter and started toward their table. She was wearing a white embroidered blouse with red cotton shorts and huaraches. Bright red clips held her long, dark brown hair off her face, revealing high cheekbones and warm brown eyes. Nancy immediately liked her.

"Buenas tardes," the petite girl greeted them with a shy smile. *"Qué quieren?"*

"I'm not what I want yet," Bess said. "Do you speak English?"

"Un poco—a little," she replied in a soft voice. "I would like to speak better. That is why I get—" She paused, her cheeks reddening slightly. "I mean, that is why I *got* a job here, so that I will be speaking English with many Americans."

Nancy smiled at the girl. "You can practice your English with us anytime. I'm Nancy Drew, and this is Bess Marvin and Ricardo Perelis."

"Ricardo is Mexican, but he speaks English almost as well as I do," Bess added.

"Muy bien," the girl began eagerly. Then she caught herself and said, "That is very good. My name is Ana. Ana Perón."

Nancy liked Ana's enthusiasm and quiet warmth. Even after taking their order for cold lime sodas and a plate of fresh mangoes, the girl lingered at their table.

"Have you visited Los Angeles?" Ana asked as she placed the order pad in her apron pocket. "It is where I want to go as soon as possible."

"Why do you want to go to L.A.?" Ricardo asked.

"It is because of my brother, Ernesto," Ana said. "He lives there, and I must see him."

Nancy noticed the worried expression that crossed Ana's face. "Is something wrong?" she asked.

Ana hesitated a moment before answering. "He has been very—" She gave Ricardo a questioning glance. *"Cómo se dice 'enfermo'?"*

"Sick," Ricardo supplied.

"Oh, no," Bess said sympathetically. "What's wrong with him?"

"Ernesto says the doctors do not know," Ana replied, biting her lip. "I am sure he must be very lonely without me. Our mother and father were killed in a crash of an automobile when we were very young, and we were raised by our aunt and uncle here in San Miguel," she explained. "Ernesto went to the United States five years ago because he could get work there in a Mexican restaurant. He has friends, but now that he is sick"—Ana shook her head—"I am afraid he will not get better without me."

"Sounds as if he should come back here so you can take care of him," Bess commented.

"I wish he could! But Ernesto is afraid that"—Ana seemed to catch herself before continuing—"if he leaves the country, his friends will not save his job for him."

"Well, maybe you could go visit him," Nancy suggested.

Ana suddenly seemed nervous. "Oh, I— There are s-some problems," she stuttered.

Nancy exchanged a look with Bess. What had made Ana so jittery all of a sudden? "Ana, is there some reason—"

"Nancy, look!" Bess interrupted in an urgent whisper, nodding to the left.

Following Bess's gaze, Nancy saw that Luis Diaz had paused at the entrance to the courtyard. As she watched, he reached into his shoulder bag and pulled out a small manila envelope, then glanced around. A moment later he spotted Nancy.

For a moment Luis just stood there. Then, shoving the envelope back in his shoulder bag, he turned and left.

"Come on, you guys," Nancy said urgently. "This time we're not going to lose him."

"Hold our food for us, Ana!" Bess said as she, Nancy, and Ricardo jumped to their feet.

Nancy took the lead. She spotted Luis's dark ponytail and orange shirt several yards ahead of them, just before he turned right, around the corner of a stone building.

"That path goes to the courtyard by the entrance," Ricardo spoke up from behind Nancy.

He, Nancy, and Bess picked up speed. "We don't want to lose him once he's left the school," Nancy said as she got to the corner. "Just remember to—"

"Stop right there!"

The menacing voice caused Nancy to stop short as she rounded the corner. A second later Bess and Ricardo crashed into her from behind.

Luis was standing just inches in front of her, fury on his face. He shook a fist at her.

"You are ruining my life!" Luis shouted. "You had better stop—or I am going to make you very sorry you ever came to San Miguel!"

Chapter

Thirteen

Nancy took an involuntary step backward, ready to lash out with a judo kick if she had to.

"Nancy's not trying to ruin anyone's life," Bess said hotly. "Anyway, if you're involved with smuggling aliens into the U.S., you deserve to get into trouble!"

Luis was so angry that his breath came in ragged bursts. He started to raise his fist again, but Ricardo jumped forward and grabbed him. "Calm down!"

Glancing quickly around them, Nancy was relieved to see that the courtyard by the entrance was fairly empty. The few passing students didn't seem to take special notice of what they were talking about.

"I saw you in Benito Juárez Park the other night," Nancy told Luis, fixing him with a stern gaze. "I think you'd better level with us about what's going on—unless you want us to call the police."

She didn't really intend to call the police, but her threat had the effect she'd hoped for.

"No! No police," Luis said quickly. He took a few deep breaths. Then he shook free of Ricardo's grasp and said, "Okay, I admit it. Maybe I *was* going to buy a false green card, but I was only doing it so that I could be with Claire when she returns to the States for school in the fall."

"But Claire said that you could enter the U.S. legally if you two got married," Bess blurted out. Then her hand flew quickly to her mouth. "Oh! I hope you don't mind that she told us that."

"I guess it's no secret that Claire and I are in love," he admitted. "We've talked about getting married, but I don't want Claire or her parents to think that the only reason I want to marry her is to get into the States. That's why I decided to get the fake green card. The truth is, I'd rather stay in Mexico. I love San Miguel. The only reason I want to go to the States is to be with Claire."

"That is *so* romantic!" Bess breathed.

"But also very illegal," Ricardo added.

Luis gave an embarrassed nod. "It's very hard to get legal permission to stay in the U.S. except for short tourist visits," he said. "I thought that a fake green card was my only option. I would have gotten it, too, if you hadn't chased me from the park the other night," he added, glaring at Nancy. "I recognized you when you started chasing me."

As Nancy listened to Luis's explanation, dozens

of questions flew through her mind. "Luis, we need to know anything you can tell us about the people who are selling the green cards. Whoever's running the operation is also ferrying Mexicans over the border in trucks," she explained.

"It's not a crime for people to want a better life, you know," Luis said, stiffening. "Some of them come from places where they are persecuted or where they'll never have the opportunity to be anything but dirt poor."

Nancy sympathized with the plight of the people, but she also knew that it was a complicated situation. "Unfortunately, some coyotes don't care about that. They just want to make a buck, and they don't care who gets hurt," she explained.

"Those are the people we're after," Bess added.

Nancy nodded. "That's why we need to know who you were meeting the other night."

Hesitating, Luis gave his ponytail a nervous tug. "I don't know his name," he finally answered. "All the arrangements were made anonymously. About a month ago a friend of a friend gave me a number to call—"

"Can you tell us who *he* is?" Ricardo asked.

Luis shrugged. "All I know is his first name— Julio. I think he left for the U.S. already. Anyway, the first time I called the number, a person told me to leave my picture and half the money—five hundred dollars—behind a planter in the cantina, a big pot of azaleas next to the arcade as you enter the courtyard. I was told to call back again in about a week, and when I did, the arrangements were made to meet at the park, where I would exchange the rest of the money for my green card."

"We all know what happened there," Bess put in. "I bet your contact wasn't happy about being interrupted by Nancy and Joe."

Luis rolled his eyes. "That's putting it mildly. After that he became very suspicious. When I called, he said there wouldn't be another meeting. I was to leave the money in an envelope behind the planter this afternoon at exactly four-thirty and then call the number again to find out where to pick up my green card."

He let out a sigh. "When I saw you three sitting there I chickened out, and now it's almost five o'clock. The man was very clear—if I don't follow his instructions exactly, the plan is off and I lose the money I've already paid."

"Hmm," Nancy said, frowning. "Well, I think you should go back to the cantina anyway and leave the envelope. Maybe we'll be lucky and the person won't have arrived to pick it up. Bess, Ricardo, and I will go back to our table separately and watch to see if anyone comes for the envelope."

Luis agreed. He started off ahead of them for the cantina, but Nancy held him back. "One more thing—I'd like to have that number you called. In case today's plan backfires, we can use it to track down the people in the smuggling ring. And, Luis"—Nancy leveled a sober gaze at him—"you have to promise not to keep trying to get the fake green card."

He hesitated slightly, then said, "I promise." He

wiped the sweat from his forehead. "To tell you the truth, this is a relief. Claire and I will have to work out something else."

After writing down the number on a slip of paper, Luis handed it to Nancy, then headed back to the cantina alone. Nancy, Ricardo, and Bess waited until after he returned to where they were standing. With a simple nod, he went past them toward the street. Then Nancy led the way back to their table.

"You are back," Ana said, coming over to them. "I was not sure if I must clear your table."

"Oh, no. We definitely want our mango," Bess said, grinning. She took a bite of the moist, orange fruit. "Mmm. It's delicious."

It took only a second for Nancy to spot the planter. It was in a shadowy area by the entrance. She could see the tiniest corner of Luis's envelope sticking out behind the planter, so she knew no one had picked it up yet.

Ricardo took a long sip of lime soda, then asked, "What do we do now?"

"We wait," Nancy replied.

An hour later the plate of mango was empty, and the teens were waiting to receive their third sodas from Ana.

"It's after six, Nan," Bess said. "Maybe Luis's contact was serious about calling off the deal. No one's been anywhere near that planter."

"I know. And we have to go soon to get ready for that dinner at the Obermans'," Nancy added. "I hate to just leave, though."

Ricardo leaned across the table to tap Nancy on the arm. "I know what to do. I'll stay here until the cantina closes. That way, if someone comes for that envelope, I'll see the person."

"You're sure you don't mind?" Nancy asked.

Turning to Bess, he said, with a teasing smile, "I would not do this for just anyone. But for my favorite American girl . . ." He leaned over to kiss the tip of Bess's nose. "I would be happy to."

"Thanks! For the favor *and* the compliment," Bess said, grinning back.

"That'll be great, Ricardo," Nancy chimed in. "Still, I'd like to do more than play this waiting game." She reached into her shorts pocket and pulled out the slip of paper Luis had given her with the phone number of his contact. For a long moment she just stared at it.

"Nancy, you're looking at that number as if it could tell you the secrets of the universe," Bess joked.

"I just need it to tell me the secrets of a certain criminal ring that's helping illegal aliens into the U.S.," Nancy said with a laugh. "Ricardo, before we go, could you do us one more favor?"

Holding up a finger, Ricardo said, "I think I can guess. I am about to become someone who needs to cross the border into the States."

"You've got the idea," Nancy said, and laughed again.

She was handing the piece of paper across the table when Ana appeared with a tray of sodas. "Three more lime sodas," she announced, smiling as she placed a glass on the table in front of Nancy. "You must be very thirsty today—"

The girl broke off as her gaze fell on the slip of

paper Nancy was passing to Ricardo. Ana's face went completely white, and her hand froze in midair.

"Ana, what is it?" Bess asked, looking concerned. "Are you all right?"

Ana shook herself. "It is nothing," she said, but Nancy noticed that her hands shook as she served the other two glasses. She wouldn't look anyone in the eye. Then she turned and hurried back to the counter.

"What was *that* all about?" Bess asked as Ricardo left to use the phone.

Nancy looked toward the kitchen area, where Ana was madly wiping the counter. "Seeing that phone number made her really nervous. She definitely recognized it."

"You think she's involved with the smugglers?" Bess asked, her blue eyes widening. "I don't believe it! She's too sweet."

"Well, she knows something. I'm sure of it," Nancy said. "And she's pretty desperate to see her brother in L.A. Maybe we can get her to open up somehow."

She looked up as Ricardo sat back down in his seat. "It's all arranged!" he said in an excited whisper.

"What's arranged? Did you talk to someone?" Nancy asked.

Ricardo nodded. "I made a rendezvous for tomorrow morning. At ten o'clock sharp, I am supposed to drop off five hundred U.S. dollars with a photograph behind the statue of the Virgin Mary at the Parroquia."

"The Parish Church, across from el Jardín. That's the place you took my picture when we first got here, Bess," Nancy said. "But wait a minute—how are you going to get that kind of money on a Saturday night?"

Ricardo gave her a confident smile. "My father does a lot of business in U.S. dollars, so he always keeps at least that much around. I am sure he won't mind us using it for a good cause."

"You're sure?" Nancy asked doubtfully. When he nodded, she shrugged and said, "Okay. We'll stake out the church. When the person comes to pick it up, we can follow him. We'll recover the money and catch some serious bad guys maybe."

"This is exactly the break we've been waiting for!" Bess exclaimed. "The Obermans will be happy to hear—" She broke off as she looked at her watch. "Yikes! It's after six-thirty. We've got to get ready for their dinner party!"

"I feel as if we've seen every pre-Columbian art dealer in Mexico City," Joe grumbled. "Are you sure Cole went into all these places?"

"No, I'm just doing this because I thought you'd enjoy seeing eight billion pre-Columbian masks," Frank answered, rolling his eyes. "What can I say? Ramirez was at his apartment, so we couldn't check it out. This seemed like the logical next step."

After leaving the bazaar, he and Joe had gone to Juan Ramirez's address. It turned out to be an apartment building. The guard himself answered when Frank and Joe rang his intercom, so they hadn't gone up or said anything. They stayed nearby watching the building, but after a few hours, they'd decided to follow up on their other clues.

For the rest of the afternoon, they'd been retracing the path Cole had taken after leaving the Galería Perelis the day before. At each stop they'd given the same pitch, saying that they were journalists doing an article on pre-Columbian masks and that they wanted to interview experts in the field. They'd managed to work Quentin Cole's name into every conversation. Although gallery owners admitted to doing business with the art collector, none of them made a single slip that would indicate Cole's involvement in anything illegal.

Of course, he and Joe hadn't expected that anyone would openly admit to knowing about anything illegal. But most gallery owners had been only too happy to show off their collections in the hopes of getting featured in their "article." Often the Hardys were taken into back rooms to see items not currently featured by the gallery, and that provided them with the perfect opportunity to snoop around.

Frank paused on the sidewalk and shaded his eyes, staring at the Galería Santos. "At least this is the last place. We'll use the same story here, okay?" he said to Joe. "You keep the owner busy while I look around."

"Sure," Joe agreed, fanning himself with his hand. "Even if we don't find anything, the air-conditioning will be a relief."

Inside, Frank and Joe found themselves in a small gallery that was exhibiting terra-cotta figures of men, women, and some animals Frank couldn't identify. The figures were on small pedestals lining three walls of the gallery. Sitting behind a desk set in front of the fourth wall was a man wearing navy slacks and a short-sleeved shirt that strained against the bulge of his stomach. His suit jacket was hung over the back of his chair.

"Buenas tardes," the man greeted them with a lazy smile.

After making sure the man spoke English, Joe launched into his story about their article.

"Ah! You have certainly come to the right place. I have been buying and selling pre-Columbian masks for over twenty-five years. Xavier Santos," the man introduced himself, shaking hands with Frank and Joe. "What magazine are you writing for?"

"Fine Arts magazine," Frank spoke up, giving the phony name he and Joe had come up with. "It's a new publication."

The man seemed skeptical. "Mmm," he said slowly, thrumming his fingers on the desk. "In my office I have slides and newspaper articles of the Galería Santos's exhibits. Wait here, and I will get anything I have on pre-Columbian masks." He opened a door set into the wall next to the desk and disappeared through it, leaving the door ajar.

Two quick steps took Frank to the doorway. Peering through it, he saw a hallway with a few doors off it. Santos went through the door at the end of the hallway.

"Keep a watch for him," Frank whispered to Joe. "I'm going to check out the other two rooms."

In a flash Frank had entered the hallway and

slipped behind the first door, which he closed behind him. He groped along the wall next to the door until he found a light switch and flicked it on.

He found himself in a storeroom lined with shelves and filled with wooden crates. The wooden lids of some of the crates had been pried open, revealing straw packing and stone or clay items. Frank saw a stone carving of a creature that looked like an eagle sticking out from one box.

"Psst!" Joe hissed from the hallway. "Hurry up! He'll be back any second."

There was no time for a thorough search, but Frank didn't see any objects made of gold or precious metals. He was about to leave when he spotted something green behind one of the crates.

"Frank!" Joe's whisper was even more urgent now, but Frank didn't answer. He stepped around the crate—then stopped short in amazement.

"Pieces of jade fitted together—turquoise along the tail," he murmured, recalling the details from the catalog Mr. Perelis had shown him.

Frank's voice was hoarse with excitement as he called to his brother in the hallway. "Joe! I've found the jade mask!"

Chapter

Fourteen

"WHAT!" Joe's mouth fell open. Abandoning his watch, he vaulted into the storeroom. There, behind a box on the floor, was a foot-high jade mask of a monkey with bits of turquoise along the tail.

"Amazing!" he breathed. "I never thought—"

The door behind them banged sharply against the wall, and the brothers whirled around. Xavier Santos was standing there, his face red with anger. "What are you doing in here? I ought to call the police!"

"That would be fine with us," Frank shot back. He pointed to the jade mask. "That mask was stolen from a friend of ours yesterday. I'm sure the police will be happy to learn that it's turned up here."

The gallery owner glanced briefly at the mask, then threw back his head and laughed. "What a joke!"

Joe shot his brother a quick look. "Mind telling us what's so funny?" he asked, crossing his arms over his chest. "'Cause from where I'm standing it looks like you're in big trouble."

"Ah, me." Xavier Santos finally stopped laughing. Moving past the Hardys, he picked up the jade mask and showed it to them. "The joke is that this mask is not real. It's an imitation."

"What!" Frank and Joe both said at once.

The gallery owner nodded. "My brother-in-law sells them to tourists at the Bazar Sábado. These stones are not real jade. They're colored soapstone. And you can see that the pieces do not fit together very well—it is obviously the work of an amateur."

Taking a closer look, Joe saw that the gallery owner was right. "Great detective work, Frank," he muttered under his breath.

"You two *journalists* have a lot to learn," Santos said dryly.

Since their cover was broken, they might as well tell the owner the truth, Frank thought. "Look, we're just trying to help our friend recover the mask," Frank said. "We think it's possible that Quentin Cole was involved in the theft. Do you know anything about that? We saw Cole come in here yesterday," he added.

Xavier Santos ushered Frank and Joe back into the gallery's showroom. "Quentin Cole is a business associate," Santos began, sitting back down at his desk. "I am aware that there are—suspicions concerning him and some recent art thefts, but if he is behind this one, he said nothing of it to me."

There was no way to know whether or not the man was lying. "Thanks for cooperating with us," Frank said. Then he and Joe left.

"Well, we made a great impression in there," Joe said sarcastically as soon as they were outside. "Let's face it. If Quentin Cole is our guy, he's extremely slippery."

Frank nodded. "But the thief did leave a calling card—the tin ornament," he reminded Joe. "That's one clue we haven't had a chance to follow up on yet."

"That's right!" Joe pulled a piece of folded paper from his wallet. "I have the address of the place that makes them right here." He held up his hand to hail a cab. "Let's go!"

A half hour later the taxi let Frank and Joe out in front of a long, low stucco building in an industrial area on the outskirts of Mexico City. Bombillas was spelled out in faded red letters above the door.

"Let's hope we have better luck here than we did at the galleries," Frank said.

While Frank asked their taxi driver to wait, Joe loped up the cement walk to the building and went in the entrance. Inside, Joe stopped to look around.

Beyond a small counter in front of him, he saw some long tables piled with tin ornaments that were being separated and packed into boxes by workers. Farther back in the long, narrow space, Joe could see other workers making and painting the ornaments.

"Does anyone run this place?" Frank asked,

coming up beside Joe. "Oh—here comes someone."

A short man wearing a sweat-stained, baggy, short-sleeved shirt over worn pants was wheeling a dolly loaded with cardboard boxes toward the entrance. He gave Frank and Joe a disinterested glance while he unloaded the boxes right next to them. Then, without saying anything, he began to wheel the dolly away.

"Excuse me," Joe called out. *"Por favor, señor?"* The man turned around slowly, giving the Hardys a blank look. "Can you help us, please?"

The man let go of the dolly, then walked slowly over to Frank and Joe, wiping his hands on his pants. *"No hablo inglés. Qué quieren?"*

"We're trying to find out if—" Joe began, but Frank cut him off. "I'll handle this."

Joe shoved his hands in the pockets of his jeans and listened while Frank talked to the man in Spanish. He didn't understand much of what they were saying, but after a few moments the man went over to one of the tables and brought back a tin ornament, which he handed to Frank.

"That's it!" Joe said, staring at the hand-shaped piece of tin. "It's the same as the calling card the thief left at Mr. Perelis's gallery."

Frank nodded. "Apparently the police were here earlier, asking about these same ornaments."

The man kept talking to Frank, and suddenly something he said made Frank more excited. Turning to Joe, Frank explained, "Our friend here says that the company is usually very slow this time of year. Their busy season is in the fall, before Christmas. But get this—he sold a box of three hundred of those hand ornaments three days ago!"

"You're kidding! Did you find out who bought them?"

"Not yet." Turning back to the man, Frank said something else in Spanish. When the man merely shrugged, Frank made gestures to describe a tall man with blond hair. "Quentin Cole," Frank finished. "Do you recognize that name?"

The man shrugged again. *"Un anglo. No sé nada más."*

"I got his drift," Joe cut in as Frank opened his mouth to translate. "The guy doesn't remember the man's description, but we do know that the buyer was an English-speaking person. I bet anything that it was Cole. Come on, let's get out of here."

Frank nodded and slipped the ornament into his pocket. "He said I could have this one," Frank explained. "We might as well go to Mr. Perelis's gallery and fill him in on what's happened."

After thanking the man, the brothers left. As their taxi started back toward the city center, Joe noticed that Frank was staring moodily out the window.

"It could have been Cole, but again, we can't *prove* that it was." Frank took a deep breath and let it out in a rush. "This guy definitely doesn't make a lot of slip-ups." Turning to Joe, he added, "Maybe Mr. Perelis was able to track down the address we found in Ramirez's locker."

The Galería Perelis was buzzing with people

when Frank and Joe got there. "There must be over fifty people here," Joe said as he and Frank headed into the main gallery.

Frank grimaced as a photographer snapped a photo of the empty pedestal where the jade mask had been. "Too bad half of them look like reporters." He nodded to the rear of the gallery, where Mr. Perelis was talking with a man in a business suit. As soon as he saw Frank and Joe, Mr. Perelis excused himself and went over to the Hardys.

"Any luck?" he asked expectantly. The hopeful gleam in his eyes faded as Frank and Joe explained that their main leads hadn't led to anything concrete.

"I see," Mr. Perelis said quietly. "That is it, then. I am ruined." He nodded to the two men he had just been talking to. "This collector is insisting on removing his piece from the exhibition. Nothing I can say will change his mind."

Joe knew the situation was desperate. If they didn't find the thief soon, Mr. Perelis's career would be totally destroyed!

"Any news from the police?" Frank asked.

"A detective called to say that they could find no concrete evidence linking the ornament to Quentin Cole, or any clue to the thief's identity," Mr. Perelis said wearily. "I should have known that Cole would be impossible to catch. He has already eluded the police many times."

"What about the address we found on the matchbook in Juan Ramirez's locker?" Joe asked.

"It is for a gallery in Los Angeles," Mr. Perelis

replied. "Five Star. I know this place, and they have nothing to do with pre-Columbian art. They deal exclusively with contemporary works." He stiffened slightly, then added, "I will ask Juan about it when he comes to work tomorrow morning."

"Señor Perelis?"

Joe turned to see the young woman from the front desk standing just behind him and Frank.

"There is a phone call for Señor Hardy," the young woman said. "He did not say which one."

"I'll take it," Joe said. He followed the receptionist back to the front desk. "Hello?"

The voice on the other end sounded muffled, as if the caller was holding a handkerchief over the mouthpiece. "I know who stole the jade mask."

"What?" Joe asked, gripping the receiver more tightly. "Who is this?"

"I can help you get the mask back," the person went on, without answering Joe's question. "Meet me at the floating gardens at Xochimilco at nine o'clock tonight."

"Hey, wait a minute!" Joe began, but the caller had already hung up. Slamming down the receiver, Joe turned to the receptionist. "Do you know who that person was?" he asked.

She shook her head. "He didn't say. Sorry."

Joe returned to where Frank and Mr. Perelis were standing. He repeated what the caller had said.

"Cole and Ramirez both know we're on this case," Frank said. "This could be a trap."

"It's also a lead, and we can't afford not to follow up," Joe pointed out. Seeing the dubious look on

133

Mr. Perelis's face, he promised, "We'll be careful. This time no one's going to get the better of Frank and Joe Hardy."

"So Luis *was* going to buy a fake green card? I can't believe it!" Claire exclaimed.

She had been in the middle of changing for dinner when Nancy and Bess found her in her room and told her about their afternoon.

"At least his intentions were good," Bess said. Nancy and Bess were sharing a room down the hall, but they were so late that they decided to change in Claire's room. That way they could tell her what had happened. Bess put on a striped blouse. "I mean, he did it for love."

Claire's cheeks reddened as she finished tucking a blue sleeveless top into matching pants. "Actually, it's a relief that he won't be able to go through with his plan. And I've been thinking of another way for us to stay together," she said softly.

Before Nancy could ask her what it was, Claire added, "And Luis *did* help us by giving us that phone number. I just hope we catch the person at the church tomorrow."

Nancy shook the wrinkles out of her sleeveless blue dress. "The person who picks up the envelope might not be the ringleader," she pointed out. "That's why we're going to follow him."

"Maybe the ringleader is Sam Breslin," Bess suggested, zipping up her white skirt and staring at her reflection in the mirror on the back of Claire's door. "He did rent all those trucks from Rápidex."

"I definitely have to check him out," Nancy said

as she slipped her dress over her head. "Let's take him up on his offer to visit his studio—"

Nancy suddenly broke off and held a finger to her lips. Was that a noise she'd just heard outside Claire's door?

She took a step closer, and a second later she heard it again—a soft thud.

It sounded as if someone was right outside Claire's door!

Chapter

Fifteen

NANCY STRODE QUICKLY to the door and yanked it open—then gaped at the tall man who was bent close to the doorway.

"Mr. Breslin!" she gasped.

"Oh!" The sculptor straightened up and stepped away. His shaggy brown hair had been combed back, and he was wearing a jacket over his lightweight slacks and shirt. For the briefest moment Nancy detected a nervous twitch beside his mouth, but it was quickly replaced by an easygoing smile. "Please, I thought I told you to call me Sam. You're Nancy, right?" Glancing past her, he nodded warmly to Claire and Bess.

Claire was apprehensive as she stepped over to the teacher. "Um, hi, Sam. What are you doing here?"

"I'm here for the dinner party," Sam explained. "I was just going to use the bathroom. I thought I remembered that it was here, but obviously I was wrong."

"It's down there, to the right," Bess directed, pointing down the hallway. As soon as the teacher had disappeared, Bess turned to Nancy and whispered, "Whoa! Do you think he heard us?"

"I don't buy his story about the bathroom," Claire added. "He's been here a zillion times. He definitely knows which room to go to."

Nancy frowned. "If he did overhear us, he didn't show any sign of it. I'll be interested to see how he reacts when your dad brings up Rápidex, Claire." After returning from Mexico City, the girls had filled in Mr. and Mrs. Oberman on their visit to the company. Since Sam Breslin had been invited for dinner anyway, Mr. Oberman had promised to see what he could find out about the sculptor's association with the trucking company.

After putting on their makeup, the girls joined the Obermans, Sam Breslin, and two women Nancy didn't recognize in the living room, an open space off the courtyard. A long couch and two chairs were upholstered in earth tones that complemented the room's wooden coffee table and chairs. Paintings and sculptures added a touch of elegance.

"I love the way I feel as if I'm out in a garden even when I'm inside," Bess said, gesturing to the potted flowers and vines in the courtyard.

"Many houses in San Miguel are built with most rooms surrounding a courtyard," Mr. Oberman explained. "In such a warm climate, it makes sense. The courtyard cools things down."

Mrs. Oberman was lighting candles on a glass-topped table that was set up in the courtyard. "The evening breeze is so nice that we'll eat out here," she called to the others. "We can sit down after everyone's acquainted."

Mr. Oberman introduced Nancy and Bess to the two women, both teachers from the institute. Leigh Carson, a painting instructor, was a willowy woman in her sixties. A long gray braid hung down her back, and Nancy thought she looked exotic in her flowing caftan. The other guest, Marlene Boyce, was in her thirties, with dark skin and black hair. She worked in the sculpture department with Sam.

As everyone talked over appetizers, Nancy had a hard time keeping her mind focused on the conversation. She kept eyeing Sam Breslin, but he didn't act the least bit uncomfortable or guilty.

It wasn't until they were halfway through their dinner of baked chicken with mango that Mrs. Oberman brought up the subject Nancy had been waiting for.

"Our upcoming student sculpture show ought to be a good one," she began. "I like the idea of placing student works beside older pieces in the same artistic tradition."

"Oh, yes," Marlene Boyce said after swallowing a bite of her chicken. "Some of my students have been working with Aztec and Mayan themes, so we're going to include some pre-Columbian sculpture beside the student works. The effect ought to be exciting."

"I suppose you'll be using Rápidex to truck the pieces here," Mr. Oberman put in innocently.

Sam Breslin nodded, then took a quick sip of his wine. "They're the best. I've been using Rápidex quite a lot lately."

At least he wasn't trying to hide the fact that he'd used their trucks, Nancy reflected. Keeping her tone light, she asked him, "Oh? What for?"

"Artwork!" Sam exclaimed, throwing his hands up in a helpless gesture. "I've been here for over ten years, and I seem to have accumulated more pieces than my studio can handle."

"I know how *that* is," Leigh Carson put in with a throaty laugh. "My studio is overflowing."

"Well, I finally decided to do something about it. I've shipped a lot of pieces to a storage facility near the gallery in the States where I exhibit," Sam explained.

Something about his explanation didn't seem quite right to Nancy. "Why not send it all up at one time?" she asked him.

Sam's hazel eyes flickered, but only for an instant. "I guess I'm the kind of guy who cleans house in fits and starts. Every time the mood hits, I clear out what I can and have it trucked north," he explained. Turning to Mrs. Oberman, he said, "This chicken is delicious, Helen."

He was clearly putting an end to the conversation, but Nancy wasn't satisfied with his answers. She would have to see for herself whether Sam Breslin's studio really had been cleared out—or whether the real reason he had hired those trucks was to ferry illegal aliens across the border into the United States.

"Mom? Dad?" Claire said, after the teachers from the institute had left. "Can I talk to you for a second?" She was helping her parents clear the table while Nancy and Bess began washing dishes in the kitchen sink.

Mrs. Oberman set some glasses down on the blue tiled counter. "Sure, honey. What is it?"

"It's about Luis," Claire began.

Mr. Oberman dropped a pile of plates on the counter with a bang. "Claire, I thought I made it very clear that—"

"I know, I know," Claire interrupted, holding up a hand. "That's why I wanted to talk to you. I'm crazy about Luis, but I decided that you're right— one summer *isn't* long enough to decide that we should spend our lives together."

"Well, honey, I think that's very sensible. . . ." Mrs. Oberman began, surprised.

"I'm not going to stop dating him," Claire went on firmly. "But we've decided that it's not— practical for him to try to come back to the States with me in the fall, either."

Nancy was dying to find out what Claire had in mind.

"That's why I've decided to transfer here to the institute as a full-time student," Claire announced. She took a deep breath and waited expectantly for her parents' reaction. "So, what do you think?"

"Claire, that's a great idea!" Bess exclaimed, "That way you guys don't have to rush into anything. . . ." She hesitated when she became aware of Mr. and Mrs. Oberman. "Uh, I guess this isn't really my business."

For a moment Mr. Oberman regarded his daughter soberly. Then he smiled. "Your mother and I will be happy to see more of you. And the institute is as good as any art school in the U.S."

"David," Mrs. Oberman said, chastising her husband and patting him on the shoulder. "What your dad is trying to say, Claire, is that we heartily approve."

Nancy couldn't help smiling as Claire hugged both her parents. It was nice to know that they had resolved their problems. Now, if only she could be as lucky in solving this case!

Frank stood on the dock at Xochimilco. It was dark, but a few tin lamps lit up the dozen or so flat-bottomed wooden boats that were tied to the long dock. With their brightly painted wooden canopies, they resembled open-air houseboats. A quarter moon above sent highlights shimmering over the water, and Frank could hear talking and singing coming from the boats floating nearby.

"According to our guidebook, there is actually a maze of canals out here," Frank said, nodding toward the dark, shadowy humps of vegetation that grew thick around the water's edge and created islands he could only see in inky black silhouette. "The gardens were originally made out of woven branches that were covered with dirt and planted with vegetables and flowers and stuff."

"Very interesting, but I'm not in the mood for a

botany lesson right now. We're here to meet someone, remember?" Joe put in. He frowned out at the water. "How are we going to find our guy?"

Frank shrugged. "I guess we'll have to wait until he finds us. This dock is pretty deserted, so I say we head out on the water."

Ten minutes later Frank sat on the deck of the flat-bottomed boat while Joe piloted it from the front end, using a long wooden pole about twelve feet long. As they moved slowly through the water, Frank scoured the faces in every boat they passed. "So far it just looks like families out for an evening of fun," he said to Joe in a low voice.

"Let's move farther out," Joe suggested. Using his pole, he steered the boat away from the crowd, toward one of the canals. Here it was quiet and deserted, almost ominous. Frank heard the water lapping against the boat and the hiss of the wind in the floating gardens. Something about the relative quiet made him tense with anticipation.

"Come on," he muttered under his breath.

Up ahead he spotted the dark silhouette of another boat that was emerging from one of the canals. As the boat drew near, Frank automatically scanned the passengers.

"That's funny," he whispered, gazing at the empty front end of the boat. "Hey, Joe, do you see anyone in there?"

Joe squinted, then shook his head. "I can't see the whole boat, though. It's too dark."

As Joe poled closer, Frank willed his eyes to penetrate the black gloom shrouding the boat. It wasn't until the two boats were about six feet apart that Frank finally spotted the dark, stocky silhouette of a man emerge from the shadow of the boat's canopy. The man was walking forward, holding the boat's steering pole out of the water. Maybe he was just moving to the front of the boat to resume poling there, or—

"Joe, watch it!" Frank cried, jumping up.

The man on the other boat suddenly raced forward, holding the long wooden pole straight out in front of him. He swung it in a low arc—aimed right at Joe's head!

Chapter

Sixteen

As JOE SPUN AROUND, he saw a man's silhouette and the deadly black streak of a weapon rushing straight at his head.

In that second he thought, My life is over.

He didn't even realize he'd dropped to the deck until he heard the attacker's pole *swoosh* through the air inches above him, then smash into the boat's wooden canopy.

"Whoa! That was close!" The sudden assault jolted Joe into a state of hyperawareness. He automatically assumed a defensive crouch as the man on the other boat retrieved his lance for another blow. Tense with anticipation, Joe peered into the black shadows of the canopy behind the attacker, searching out any other threatening movement. At the same time he groped wildly for their boat's guiding pole, which he'd dropped to the deck.

Before he could find it, the attacker's lance came whipping through the air again, this time cutting low.

Joe jumped, then yelled with pain as he felt the pole hit the lower part of his legs. The impact sent him flipping sideways, and the next thing he knew, he was plunging headfirst into the water.

"Joe!" Frank caught a glimpse of Joe thrashing in the water, but there was no time to help his brother. Frank leapt forward and grabbed their boat's guiding pole from the deck. He thrust it at their attacker. The man was able to deflect the blow using his own lance.

Frank struck again. Again the man deflected the blow. Then he swung wildly, but Frank was prepared. He hit the man's pole as hard as he could. The sound of wood hitting wood echoed across the water, but still the attacker held on to his pole.

Out of the corner of his eye, Frank saw that Joe was moving stealthily toward the other boat. Frank knew he had to keep his attacker's attention.

"Come and get me," Frank taunted, holding his arms wide open. "What's the matter, are you afraid to go face-to-face with us?"

Frank heard the man's throaty growl a second before the other wooden lance came smashing toward him. With one swift motion, Frank arced his own pole out. This time he hit the other man's pole with such force that he knocked it into the water. Then, using the pole like a sword, he jabbed the man in the abdomen. The man reeled back into the shadow of the canopy.

"Way to go!" Joe called as he pulled himself out of the water and onto the deck of the other boat. Frank couldn't see what was happening. Joe disappeared into the opaque darkness beneath the wooden canopy.

Quickly Frank poled closer. Then when the boats were only a few feet apart, Frank, still holding the pole, jumped to the other deck. He expected to hear a struggle, but there was only silence.

"Joe?" Frank tried to fight back the edginess that crept over him. He quickly bent beneath the wooden canopy, keeping the wooden pole primed to fight off an attack. But as his eyes adjusted to the blackness, he saw only one person, crouching low over the bottom of the boat.

"The guy disappeared!" Joe said, squeezing water from his shirt as he straightened up.

Frank dropped the pole to the deck, then raced to the rear of the boat. "He must have jumped overboard," he said. He searched the water's surface, but didn't see or hear anyone swimming.

"I don't believe this," Joe said. His sopping wet sneakers made squishing noises as he came up beside Frank. "He got away again!"

Frank noticed the emphasis his brother placed on "again." "I thought he looked familiar, too," Frank said. "He had the same build as that one-man mariachi death squad we met at the bazaar."

"Juan Ramirez?" Joe asked.

Frank sank down onto one of the chairs beneath the boat's canopy. "Could be."

"But we still don't know for sure," Joe added. "I'm sick of running into dead ends all the time! I say we head back to Quentin Cole's hotel and lay our cards on the table. I know he's mixed up in this—I can feel it."

"I don't know, Joe," Frank said, hesitating. "Cole's too tall to have been our attacker, and—"

Joe held up a hand. "I know it's a long shot, but do you have a better idea?"

Frank was going to object, but he only shrugged and said, "It's worth a shot."

It took over an hour to return their boat to the dock and take a taxi back to the center of Mexico City. By the time they reached the Villa Flores, it was almost eleven o'clock.

"You're sure you don't want to head back to the Perelises' and get into some dry clothes?" Frank asked as their cab pulled up at the inn.

Joe shook his head and held out some damp peso notes to the driver, then hopped out onto the sidewalk. "I'm getting used to the wet look."

As they went through the inn's wrought-iron gate, Joe saw the same dark-haired woman behind the reception counter. This time he and Frank didn't even bother to distract her.

"Good, Cole's light's on," Frank said as they went up the spiral staircase.

They knocked on the door to room 24. "Come on out. It's Frank and Joe Hardy," Joe said loudly. "We want to talk to you."

Joe heard the murmur of voices inside. A moment later the door opened a crack. A middle-aged woman peeked out. Her graying hair was in curlers,

147

and she was clutching a light robe to her throat. *"Sí?"* she asked, eyeing the Hardys suspiciously.

Frank said to the woman, "We want to talk to Quentin Cole. This is his room, right?"

The woman stared blankly at Frank. Before he or Joe could say anything more, they heard the tapping of someone coming up the wrought-iron stairway. A second later the receptionist appeared. When she saw Frank and Joe, she frowned and started speaking rapidly in Spanish.

"It's nice to see you again, too," Joe said, turning on his most brilliant smile. "Remember us? We were just looking for our friend Mr. Cole."

The receptionist spoke placatingly to the woman for a moment, then quickly ushered Frank and Joe back down to the reception area. "Quentin Cole is not here. He checked out this morning."

"What!" Joe exclaimed. "You can't be serious."

"I am very serious," the woman said, acting more and more exasperated. "Now please, I must ask you to leave."

Joe couldn't believe it. Cole was gone. They lost their top suspect—and the jade mask—maybe for good.

"It's nine forty-five, and it looks like mass is over," Bess said to Nancy and Claire Sunday morning. "Let's go in and find a good place to observe before Ricardo shows up."

The three girls were sitting on a bench in el Jardín, gazing up at the fairytale-like Parish Church across the street. Its pale pink spires rose high into the sky, and lacy parapets and belfries gave it a fanciful appearance.

Mass had just let out, and Nancy watched families leaving the church, laughing and talking. People lingered outside talking to one another. The man who was behind the drop-off had planned well, Nancy realized. Ricardo would be entering the church before the next mass and would attract no attention.

Nancy frowned and looked around. Ever since leaving the Obermans', she'd had the feeling that they were being watched.

Take it easy, Drew, she ordered herself. So far, no one entering or leaving the church had looked at all threatening or weird. Besides, anyone who *was* watching would think they were just going to Sunday mass. "I guess it's okay to go in," she agreed, standing.

As they crossed the street, Nancy said, "Okay, when we get inside, let's find a place to wait. I want to be able to see the statue where Ricardo is supposed to leave his photo and money, but we don't want to be too conspicuous."

The inside of the church was much plainer than the outside, Nancy saw, with a wooden crucifix over the main altar, wooden benches, and stone columns that ran the length of the church along the sides. Luckily, since it was between masses, no more than half a dozen people sat in the pews.

"Nan, that must be the drop-off place," Bess whispered.

Nancy saw that Bess was pointing to a semicircular area near the rear of the church, to the right. The recessed area was dominated by a statue of the Virgin Mary wearing a blue robe. Rows of candles were laid out at the foot of the statue, and a colorful arrangement of flowers had been placed nearby, in a niche in the stone.

"We could sit in a pew at the back, on the other side of the church," Claire suggested.

"Good idea," Nancy agreed. "Right next to that pillar, so we won't stand out."

Once they were settled, Nancy tried to relax a little, but she still had that prickly feeling at the back of her neck. Something was about to happen —she could feel it—and with any luck they would have the criminals in custody very soon.

"*Psst!* You guys, there he is," Bess hissed.

Nancy saw that Ricardo had just entered the church. He didn't turn his gaze left or right, but walked over to the area where the statue was. He lit a candle and stood quietly for a moment. Then, checking that no one was watching him, he slipped an envelope behind the vase of flowers. He moved so quickly and fluidly that Nancy barely saw him do it.

"Good," Nancy whispered. "Now we wait."

Five minutes passed, then ten. Still no one came to pick up the envelope. Nancy felt as if each second dragged. "Come on," she said under her breath. "I hope this doesn't take all—"

"*Por favor, señoritas . . .*"

Nancy snapped around to her left, where the voice had come from. The woman standing beside the pew was one of the shortest, oldest people she had ever seen. She was wearing a dusty black dress and shawl that covered everything except for her face and hands. Her gnarled body was bent over the stick that she used as a cane.

"Diez pesos para una pobre vieja," the woman said, holding out her hand.

"She's asking for help," Bess said, reaching to unzip the pack strapped around her waist. "I can tell that even without understanding Spanish."

Nancy was also reaching for her wallet, when all of the sudden she remembered Ricardo's envelope and quickly checked back to the area with the statue.

"Oh, no!" she gasped.

"What's the matter?" Claire asked.

Nancy felt sick as she stared at the niche in the wall. "Ricardo's envelope—it's gone!"

Chapter

Seventeen

G ONE? IT CAN'T BE!" Bess cried, spinning around toward the candlelit area by the statue.

"It is," Nancy said. Frustration swept over her. "I only looked away for a second, but—" Her eyes narrowed as she gazed back at the beggar, who was now moving slowly toward the entrance to the church. Nancy jumped up from the pew and hurried over to the woman.

"Excuse me, ma'am. Did someone tell you to come over to us?" Nancy asked. Seeing the woman's blank expression, Nancy asked the question again in Spanish. This time the woman nodded. Nancy then asked what the person looked like, but the woman merely shook her head.

"We've been tricked," Nancy said, hurrying back

to Bess and Claire. "Come on. Maybe it's not too late to spot the person who took the envelope."

Nancy barely managed to keep herself from running as they left the church. As soon as they were outside, her eyes darted in every direction.

"Try to spot anyone holding that envelope," she called to Claire and Bess, "or anyone who looks suspicious or like—"

Nancy suddenly felt someone grab her arm and twist it behind her back. Then a commanding voice spoke up in her ear. *"Alto!* Stop right there!"

A stab of pain shot up Nancy's arm. She twisted her head around—then blinked in surprise.

"Señora Sandoval!" she exclaimed.

The cantina owner was surprisingly strong, and her expression was so fierce it frightened Nancy. She quickly pulled Nancy around to the secluded side of the church. Then, holding Nancy's arm with one hand, she reached into her leather shoulder bag with her other hand and pulled out a badge. "Police," she said. "Don't move."

"Police?" Nancy echoed, trying to make sense of the situation. "But you run the cantina at the Instituto San Miguel!" Out of the corner of her eye, she saw that Bess, Claire, and Ricardo were being detained by two male officers in plainclothes.

"The cantina is my cover," Maria Sandoval explained. "Do not pretend that you don't know what I am talking about. You are obviously involved."

"We didn't do anything!" Bess protested.

"That's right," Claire agreed. "And you're ruining our chance to find the people who've been selling green cards—" She broke off in midsentence as she realized her slip. "I guess that was supposed to be a secret, huh?"

Without loosening her grip on Nancy, Maria Sandoval turned to Claire. "Then how do you four know about the operation, unless you are mixed up in it? I knew there was something funny about you when you were asking questions at the cantina a few days ago. I finally got some backup to follow you this morning," she added, nodding curtly toward the two other officers. "And you lead us right to an illegal transaction."

"I can explain if you'll just let go of me for a minute," Nancy said over her shoulder.

Maria Sandoval finally released her grip, and Nancy turned around, rubbing her arm. As calmly as she could, she explained the situation, including all the details of her investigation so far. She finished by telling them about getting the phone number and Ricardo's arrangement to drop off his money and picture.

"We were going to follow whoever picked up the money, hoping the person would lead us to the headquarters of the ring," Nancy finished.

Rubbing her chin, Maria Sandoval gazed from Nancy to the others. "I am impressed with your thoroughness," she said, "but this is a serious police investigation. You should not interfere. The reason I instructed that beggar woman to approach you was that I saw a man in the rear of the church who appeared to be paying close attention to your envelope. If you were involved with him, I wanted to distract you so that we could follow him."

"You saw someone? Who was it?" Nancy asked. When Maria simply frowned, she said, "Was he squat and muscular, with a nose that's been broken a few times?"

Maria didn't say anything, but her surprised expression answered Nancy's question.

"It *was* him," Claire said. "The guy from Rápidex!"

"I can't believe we didn't get to follow him," Bess added.

Maria Sandoval said a few words in Spanish to the other two officers, then spoke severely to Bess. "It is not the place of civilians, especially foreign ones, to follow criminals. He could be dangerous."

"What about your people? Did they follow him?" Nancy asked.

The officer was starting to act annoyed. "When you and your friends barged out of the church, the man saw and took off. I have a man following him, but I do not think he will lead us anywhere significant today."

"Maybe next time," Nancy said hopefully. She didn't think it would be wise to say what she was really thinking—that if Maria Sandoval and her backup hadn't interrupted *them,* they could be hot on the trail of the ringleaders right now.

Later that afternoon, the girls, Claire, Ricardo, and Mr. and Mrs. Oberman were all sitting around the table in the Obermans' courtyard. Maria

Sandoval had spent the last two hours grilling them. Nancy had been dying to get more information about the police case, but Maria had been close-mouthed. After warning the group to leave the case to the police, she and the other officers finally left.

"Phew!" Bess exclaimed with relief. "I can't believe the Mexican government has had Maria Sandoval investigating this criminal ring for three months already."

"Too bad Maria wouldn't say anything more than that about her case," Nancy said.

"Except that we would all go to jail if we did anything to compromise her cover at the cantina," Claire put in.

Ricardo took a sip of the mint tea Mrs. Oberman had made, then looked at Nancy. "What do we do now, just drop everything?"

"That's exactly what we do," Mr. Oberman said sternly. "We can't risk alienating the police."

"But, Mr. Oberman, you said yourself that police bureaucracy always causes delays," Bess put in. "That could mean the criminal ring will have time to cover their tracks—especially now that they know someone is onto them."

"Or this whole thing could blow up while the academic panel is visiting," Claire added. "If the police arrest someone from the institute in some flashy bust, the panel's assessment of the school probably won't be too hot."

Mr. Oberman said soberly, "I'm afraid we can't recommend that you disobey the police. We do appreciate all you've done so far, though," he added with a weak smile. "And I hope you'll stay in

San Miguel to sightsee and enjoy yourselves." He sighed deeply, then got to his feet. "Well, Helen, we have to meet with the accountant."

Claire's parents said goodbye, leaving Nancy, Claire, Bess, and Ricardo staring glumly at one another. "So that's it? We just drop the whole thing?" Claire asked.

Nancy tapped a fingernail against her glass, thinking. "Sam Breslin *did* invite us to his studio," she pointed out. "I think it would be rude *not* to stop by. And if we happen to go there when he's not around, we might as well have a look, right?"

"Nancy, you are *so* sneaky," Bess said. "I love it!"

"Why don't we go there now?" Ricardo suggested.

"I think we'd better lay low for today," Nancy said. "Maria Sandoval and her men are probably checking up on all our suspects. If they catch us investigating, we'll be in big trouble."

"I guess you're right," Bess agreed. "Well, you guys are the local experts," she said to Claire and Ricardo. "What should we do this afternoon?"

"We could go to the hot springs at Taboada," Claire suggested.

"That's a great idea!" Ricardo agreed. "These are public baths just north of San Miguel that are fed by natural hot springs. It's a wonderful place," he said to Nancy and Bess. "Did you bring bathing suits?"

"You bet," Bess answered, grinning.

Nancy nodded. "If you guys don't mind, there's someone else I'd like to invite," she said. "Ana

Perón. After the way she reacted to seeing the phone number Luis gave us yesterday, I think she knows something."

"She seems very shy," Ricardo said dubiously.

"Not to mention afraid," Bess added. "Do you think she'll tell us anything?"

"I'm not sure," Nancy admitted. "But I want to try. I hope she's not working today. Let's call the cantina and see. If she's not there, maybe someone can tell us where she lives."

"I am very happy you invited me to accompany you to these baths," Ana Perón said an hour and a half later as she sat waist-deep in one of the large, terraced cement pools at Taboada.

"We were lucky that when we called the cantina, they had your address," Claire said, shaking the water from her red hair. "I'm glad you could come."

"Mmm. This warm water is so soothing," Bess added.

Nancy had to agree. She, Ana, Claire, Bess, and Ricardo had just gotten into the open pool, and already Nancy could feel some of the tension easing from her body. Still, she didn't want to get too relaxed—she was on a case, after all. Reluctantly, she stepped out of the water, then sat at the edge of the pool and wrapped her arms around her knees. "Ana, I was thinking about your brother, and I'd like to help you," she began.

"Yes?" Ana turned to face Nancy, her big brown eyes filled with hope. "Do you think you can? It would mean everything to me!"

"I hope I can," Nancy hedged. She'd been so busy with the case that she hadn't yet had a chance to call her dad, but she made a mental note to phone him as soon as they returned to the Obermans. "But first I was hoping *you* could help *us* with something."

Ana nodded. "Of course," she answered, smiling.

Nancy took a deep breath. "Ana, we think it's possible that someone from San Miguel is helping people enter the United States illegally," she said. "Do you know anything about that?"

The smile disappeared from Ana's face. "I—I am afraid I do not understand."

"We're not trying to get you in trouble," Claire said quickly. "But you *do* want desperately to see your brother, and we thought maybe—"

"You recognized that phone number Nancy had at the cantina the other day, didn't you?" Bess cut in gently. She placed her hand on Ana's arm, but Ana jerked away. The girl was blinking back tears now, and she looked terrified.

"N-no. I do not know what you are talking about," Ana said. With that, she ducked under the water and quickly swam to another part of the pool.

Ana obviously wasn't going to say anything more. For the rest of the afternoon, Nancy kept the conversation off the case, but when they piled back into Ricardo's car, Ana was still edgy. She seemed relieved when they got back to town.

Nancy was staring idly out the window when her gaze fell on a tall man strolling beneath the neatly trimmed Indian laurel trees. It took a moment for her to realize that she'd seen the man before.

"Ricardo, stop!" she exclaimed, leaning forward in the backseat. "We have to find a phone!"

Bess and Ana both twisted around to stare at Nancy. "What is it? What's wrong, Nan?" Bess asked.

"You're not going to believe who I just saw," Nancy said excitedly. "We have to call the Hardys right away!"

Mr. Perelis and Rosa were both at the Perelises' Mexico City apartment when Joe and Frank walked in the door late Sunday afternoon. Mr. Perelis was reading the paper on the modern chrome-and-leather couch in the living room. Rosa, eating a plate of melon in the adjoining dining room, seemed to be completely ignoring her father.

"I am sorry I missed seeing you and Frank last night, but I went to bed early and went to the gallery this morning first thing," Mr. Perelis said as Joe sat down next to him on the couch. "Since the robbery, I have added an extra guard at night, but I still go early every morning to make sure everything is all right."

Joe and Frank sat down on the matching chrome-and-leather chairs on the other side of the burnished metal coffee table.

"You are making progress? How was your rendezvous at Xochimilco?" Mr. Perelis asked.

"Yes," Rosa called from the dining room. "How *is* your investigation going?"

Joe didn't miss the sarcasm in her voice, but he decided not to take the bait. He was too busy wondering how to break the bad news to Mr. Perelis about Cole having skipped town.

He and Frank had spent the entire day trying to track down Quentin Cole. They'd called their father, hoping he could use his connections to find out whether Cole had crossed the border back into the U.S. It had taken forever to learn that there was no record of Cole entering the U.S., but that didn't mean he wasn't already in some other country or that he hadn't bypassed legal ways of crossing the border.

"Our rendezvous didn't exactly go the way we'd hoped—" Frank began.

The jangling of the phone on the desk across the room interrupted them. Mr. Perelis got to his feet, went over to the desk, and answered.

"Hola. Yes, hello, Nancy. Of course I remember you. Yes, Frank and Joe are right here. Hold on."

"I wonder what she wants?" Frank said, going over to the desk and taking the phone from Mr. Perelis. "Hi, Nancy. What's up?"

He listened quietly for a moment, and then his jaw dropped. "You're kidding! Thanks for the tip, Nancy. We'll be there as soon as we can."

"What's up?" Joe asked.

Frank replaced the receiver, then spun around to face Joe. "You're not going to believe who Nancy just spotted in San Miguel—Quentin Cole."

Chapter

Eighteen

"THANKS FOR THE COFFEE, Mrs. Oberman," Frank said Monday morning. "I can use it."

Joe nodded, stifling a yawn as he reached for the cup of *café con leche* Mrs. Oberman had placed in front of him. "By the time we got here last night, it was pretty late," he added.

The Hardys, Nancy, Bess, Claire, and Mr. and Mrs. Oberman were sitting around the table in the Obermans' courtyard for a breakfast of coffee and spicy Mexican cornbread.

"I'm ready to move, though," Joe added. "I don't want to lose Quentin Cole *again*."

"That's what we figured," Nancy said. "We followed him to his hotel yesterday. It's the Casa de Sierra Nevada, about a block from el Jardín."

162

Frank frowned into his coffee. "This could be tricky. I mean, if he has the mask—and that's something we haven't been able to prove yet—he didn't keep it with him at his hotel in Mexico City."

"So he might not have it at his hotel here, either?" Claire guessed.

Bess popped the last of her cornbread into her mouth, then reached for another piece. "So what can we do to find the mask?" she asked.

"Joe and I will still check out Cole's hotel," Frank said. "Maybe if we follow him, he'll lead us to the jade mask." Taking the tin ornament from his shirt pocket, he flipped it over and over in his hands. "I just wish we could find some connection between him and the calling card that was left at Mr. Perelis's gallery."

"The guy doesn't make a lot of mistakes," Joe said, downing the rest of his coffee. "The last time we tried to tail him, the plan backfired, remember?"

Mr. and Mrs. Oberman had been listening to the conversation. Now, Mr. Oberman tossed his napkin on the table and said, "I think what we need is a way to trick the man into making a mistake."

"A setup." Nancy nodded toward Frank and Joe. "Sounds like a good idea, but what *kind* of setup?"

"Well, we *are* having a show at the institute's gallery in a few weeks," Mr. Oberman began.

"That student sculpture show you and the teachers were talking about the other night," Bess put in.

"Yes," Mr. Oberman said. "In addition to the students' work, we're including some pre-

Columbian pieces," he said. He pushed his glasses up on his nose. "I could put out the word that one of those sculptures is a rare, silver-decorated terra-cotta figure that we're receiving on loan from the Museum of Anthropology in Mexico City. If I let slip that I'm holding the piece in my safe here at home overnight so that I can study it before moving it to our guarded facilities at the institute's museum . . ."

"Cole might not be able to resist the chance to steal the sculpture, and we could catch him in the act!" Frank finished.

"Then we'll have him over a barrel. If he has a choice between doing time here in Mexico or handing over the jade mask, I bet I know which he'll choose," Joe added.

"Wait a minute," Bess said, confused. "How are we going to get our hands on this rare terra-cotta thing?"

Mr. Oberman grinned at his wife, who rose and went into the living room. A moment later she returned holding a figure of a woman with silver ornamentation around her head. "This is an imitation," she explained, "but Quentin Cole doesn't have to know that."

"I have a friend—an art dealer who regularly does business with Quentin Cole," Mr. Oberman went on. "If I tell my friend about the terra-cotta piece, I'm sure he'll pass the news along to Cole. I'll call him right now, if you like."

Mr. Oberman's gaze took in the Hardys. The two of them reached over the table at the same time to give each other a high five, and Frank exclaimed, "Let's go for it!"

"Psst! Nancy, what time is it?" Bess hissed into the darkness of Mr. Oberman's study.

Nancy hit the button on her watch that illuminated the numbers. "Ten after one," she whispered back.

"I hope Quentin Cole shows up soon. My legs are starting to cramp up," Claire murmured. "I mean, what if he doesn't show up at all?"

"Then we'll have to come up with another plan," Nancy answered, "but I have a hunch he'll be here." She was feeling a little stiff, too, from crouching down for so long behind the sofa. They had been camped out there since just after dinner, but Nancy didn't dare move. If Cole chose that moment to arrive, their whole plan would be ruined. That is, *if* he arrived. Claire was right—there was nothing to assure that he would.

Sticking her head around the edge of the sofa, Nancy peered into the darkness. She couldn't see the Hardys, but she knew they were hiding in the study closet, with the door opened just a crack. They all had a good view of the painting behind the desk that covered Mr. Oberman's safe. If Quentin Cole was the talented thief everyone thought he was, he wouldn't have trouble locating the safe, but Frank had tipped the painting so that it was just a little crooked, to make the safe's location more obvious.

Nancy didn't know how much time had passed

when she heard it—the slightest scratching noise on the tiled floor. Nancy jolted to attention, all her senses on red alert. She couldn't see Bess or Claire's face, but Bess grabbed her arm to let her know that she had heard it, too.

When Nancy peeked around the side of the couch, she saw nothing at first. Then a penlight suddenly flicked on. Nancy ducked low behind the couch, but she could see the beam playing over the walls and furniture until it came to rest somewhere near the desk.

Without making a sound, Nancy shifted to get a better view. She could barely hear the intruder at all, but the penlight beam showed that he was moving toward the crooked painting. As he drew closer, the beam reflected off the painted surface, illuminating Quentin Cole's face. His expression, Nancy saw, was one of total concentration.

She watched him lift the painting from the wall, revealing the safe. He glanced around him before taking a headset and sensors from his inside jacket pocket. Nancy knew the device would help him hear the tumblers click into place as he located the correct numbers of the safe's combination.

After attaching the sensors to the safe and putting on the headset, he started dialing the knob at the center of the metal door. It took only a minute before Nancy heard the solid *clunk* that told her he had found the correct combination.

She could feel the tense anticipation radiating from Claire and Bess.

A moment later Nancy practically jumped out of her skin when Cole snapped his head around toward the study closet. For a long moment he stared at the door. The silence in the room pounded inside Nancy's head, and she hardly dared breathe.

It seemed to take forever before Cole finally turned back to the safe. He quickly pulled open the safe door, then shone his penlight inside. Even from behind the couch, Nancy could see the terracotta figure. As Quentin Cole reached inside carefully and took the statue out, Nancy saw him smile in satisfaction.

Nancy tensed, waiting for the Hardys to take the lead. A split second later she heard the closet door bang open.

"Hold it right there, Cole!" Joe's commanding voice rang out.

At the same time Nancy leapt to her feet and flicked on the switch by the door. Quentin Cole's eyes widened when he saw the five of them bearing down on him.

"Well, well, well," Frank said. "It looks as if we've finally caught the uncatchable thief."

Chapter

Nineteen

QUENTIN COLE FLINCHED, and for the briefest instant Joe saw panic in his pale blue eyes. Then, moving with the agility of a panther, he tucked the terra-cotta figure under his arm and leapt toward the door of Mr. Oberman's study.

"Oh, no, you don't," Joe said, jumping in front of Cole. "You can't slither out of this one."

Frank moved in and grabbed Cole by the shoulders while Joe retrieved the statue. Frank reached to pin the man's arms behind his back, but Quentin Cole shook himself free, then held up his hands.

"There's no need for manhandling," he said indignantly. Cole didn't make a move, but Joe saw the way his eyes played over the group, as if he were sizing up the situation.

"You're in serious hot water for stealing this," Joe said, holding out the terra-cotta figure.

Quentin Cole's gaze narrowed as he looked at the piece. "That worthless thing?" Cole said with a dismissive wave. "Anyone can see it's a fake."

What was this guy's game? Joe wondered. Cole's panicked expression was gone now, replaced by the arrogant nonchalance Joe recognized.

"A fake that you tried to steal by breaking into this house," Nancy pointed out, stepping over to the group. "That's still enough reason to arrest you."

"I'm going to get my parents," Claire said, running for the door to the courtyard. "I'm sure they'll call the police."

Joe waited a second for Claire's words to sink in. Then he turned to Cole and said, "It's like this. Either you tell us everything you know about the jade mask, or you go to jail."

Cole didn't even flinch. For someone who could spend time behind bars, Joe reflected, the guy seemed awfully cool, calm, and collected.

"What have we here?" Mr. Oberman asked a moment later as he and Mrs. Oberman hurried into the study, both wearing robes over their pajamas.

"We got him right after he broke into the safe and took the statue," Bess said proudly.

For a moment Cole simply gazed around the study at everyone. Then he leaned back against the desk and crossed his arms over his chest. "Let me understand," he began. "You think I stole the jade mask, and you're willing not to press charges for this theft if I return the mask to Mr. Perelis."

"Something like that," Joe said. He didn't bother to add that Cole would be doing a lot of jail time anyway for stealing the mask.

"That's quite an irresistible proposition," Cole said, acting as if they had just invited him for tea. "There's just one problem with it."

"What's that?" Frank asked.

"Well, as I'm sure you know, I'm an art collector—a *legitimate* art collector," Cole began.

Joe couldn't believe it. They had caught Cole red-handed, and he was still trying to bluff his way out of the situation. "Do *legitimate* art collectors make a habit of breaking into safes in people's homes?" he asked.

Quentin Cole appeared not to have heard Joe's question. "It seems to me that the real question is, who stole the mask?"

Joe looked at Frank. What was going on here? Why was Cole putting on this phony act?

"Let's cut to the chase, okay?" Frank said.

Cole nodded. "As you like. For argument's sake, let's say that a certain party *was* interested in obtaining the jade mask—"

"Stealing it, you mean," Nancy corrected.

"Whatever," Cole said smoothly. "It's quite possible that someone else got to the mask before this certain person was able to."

"Are you saying that someone beat you to the punch?" Frank asked.

Quentin Cole held up his hands defensively. "I'm not *saying* anything," he insisted. "I'm just presenting a theoretical possibility."

"Theoretically, are you saying that you know who the thief is?" Joe asked.

Cole gave an easy shrug. "One never knows for sure, does one?"

Joe tried to stifle his frustration. Why was it so impossible to get a straight answer out of this guy? Turning to his brother, he said, "Let's talk, Frank— in private."

"We'll make sure Mr. Cole doesn't go anywhere," Nancy volunteered.

As soon as he and Frank were in the courtyard, Joe exploded. "That guy really burns me," he said. "I'd love to put him away."

"Me, too, brother, but not now," Frank said. "Cole will be much more valuable to us if he goes free. He obviously knows who stole the mask. If we let him go, he could lead us right to the thief."

"I guess you're right, but I have a feeling Cole's not going to make this easy for us," Joe said. "Now we have to recover the jade mask before he can steal it out from under us!"

Joe was pouring himself a glass of orange juice the next morning when Rosa bounced into the kitchen of the Perelises' San Miguel home in a cotton flowered jumpsuit. Her whole face radiated cheerfulness—until she saw Joe.

"Oh. Good morning," Rosa said stiffly. She stepped past him, went to the stamped-tin bread box, and took out a roll. "You and Frank were out late last night."

Joe wasn't about to spill the details of their

confrontation with Quentin Cole. "Mmm," he said noncommittally, yawning. It was only a little after eight—Frank and Ricardo were still in bed—but Joe hadn't been able to sleep any longer. Every time he closed his eyes he saw Quentin Cole's taunting face.

Rosa turned to fix Joe with a probing stare. She acted as if she was going to ask him a question, but then she just shrugged and headed for the kitchen door. "I have to go somewhere. Ricardo will probably be up soon to keep you company. 'Bye."

With that, she left the kitchen.

Somewhere? That was awfully vague, Joe thought, staring after her. It was too early to do any kind of shopping. Maybe it was time he found out what Rosa did all these times she took off alone.

Joe downed his juice, then jumped to his feet and headed for the door. Out on the street, he looked both ways and saw Rosa heading down the hill to the right. Keeping a safe distance back, he took off after her.

He still wasn't sure what to think about Rosa. He didn't like to think that she would actually help someone steal a priceless mask from her father, but he and Frank couldn't afford to take any chances.

Up ahead, Joe saw a sign for the Casa de Sierra Nevada. "Cole's hotel," he mumbled under his breath. He paused, waiting to see if Rosa would go inside, but she walked quickly past.

For the next ten minutes, she led Joe on a route past el Jardín and beyond the outdoor market. Finally Rosa turned into a doorway and pressed a bell. The door opened a few moments later, and she disappeared inside.

Sprinting to the doorway, Joe pressed his ear to the wooden door. When he didn't hear anything, he pushed against the door, and it swung inward.

Joe held his breath, waiting for a voice to yell at him. When none did, he looked through the opening and saw a seedy courtyard with rooms around it on two floors. Weeds sprouted along the edges of the open area, and the plaster walls of the surrounding rooms were crumbling in spots. Joe saw a series of metal mailboxes just inside the front door. Apparently, this was a group of apartments.

Joe heard a door close to his right. There were three doorways on that side of the courtyard. As he approached the second one, Joe heard Rosa's voice coming through the open window next to the door.

"I came by to see you yesterday, Jim, but you were not here," Rosa was saying.

"I can't always be around when you want me to, Rosie," Jim Stanton's deep voice answered.

Joe inched closer to the window until he caught a glimpse of Rosa, sitting at a red kitchen table. Stanton poured her a cup of coffee, then sat down.

"Did you miss me while I was away?" Rosa asked.

It was odd the way Rosa lost her flip, rebellious attitude around Stanton, Joe reflected. She obviously wanted to please him, but from what Joe could see, Stanton didn't seem to care.

Stanton's angular features seemed to stiffen a little. "I've been busy, okay? Stop hounding me."

"Fine," Rosa said, beginning to sound annoyed. "I guess I am finding out why your nickname is *el Conejo*. It is because—"

"Don't ever call me that!" Jim burst out.

Joe shifted uneasily as Rosa said something placating. He was beginning to wish he hadn't followed Rosa. It was embarrassing to hear such a personal fight. It obviously didn't have anything to do with the stolen jade mask, so Joe moved quickly out to the street.

He glanced at his watch. It was almost nine. As they had planned the night before, Frank and Ricardo had probably just left to stake out Cole's hotel. Joe hoped Cole hadn't skipped town *again*.

He was on his way to join his brother and Ricardo, when his growling stomach reminded him that he hadn't had anything to eat yet. He changed his route, heading back toward the Perelises' instead. The stakeout could wait for a few minutes— his stomach definitely could not.

"Am I really awake and walking around after just four hours of rest, or am I sleepwalking?" Bess asked Nancy and Claire as they stepped out of the Obermans' front door and started down the street.

"I hate to hit you over the head with reality, but you're awake," Nancy said, stifling a yawn. They hadn't gotten to bed until after two-thirty the night before, and she was tired as well.

Bess groaned. "That's what I was afraid of."

Claire gave them an apologetic smile and said, "Sorry, guys. I guess I shouldn't have made plans to meet Luis for breakfast. It's just that I haven't had a

chance to really talk to him since we straightened
out all this green card stuff, and—"

"Don't worry about it," Bess said quickly. "It'll
be nice to be relaxed around him now that we don't
have to think of him as a suspect."

"Anyway, I'm glad to get an early start today,"
Nancy said. "We were so caught up in helping
Frank and Joe yesterday that we didn't have a
chance to work on our own investigation."

"The academic review board arrives today,"
Claire said soberly. "I just hope the whole case
doesn't blow up in our faces while they're here."

The three girls were just passing the entrance to
the institute when Nancy saw Maria Sandoval
hurrying down the street toward them. A white
apron was slung over her leather shoulder bag, and
she appeared distraught.

"Señora Sandoval, is something wrong?" Nancy
asked, when they came face to face.

The older woman blinked, as if she'd only just
noticed the girls. "I suppose it cannot hurt to tell
you . . ."

"What?" Claire asked. "Is it about the case?"

"My superior in Mexico City called me this
morning. The border patrol caught a truckload of
people trying to sneak across the border."

"Was it a Rápidex truck?" Nancy guessed.

Maria Sandoval nodded. "The truck was crossing
the border between checkpoints," she explained.
"When the border patrol tried to stop them, the
truck's driver ran. Unfortunately, he did not bother
to stop his truck before he jumped out and took
off."

"How awful!" Bess exclaimed. "What happened to all the people in the truck?"

The woman's eyes burned with anger as she spoke. "The truck ran off the road and into a ravine. Two people died, and several others were seriously hurt."

Nancy felt as if she had been punched in the stomach.

"The crime we are investigating is not just smuggling people illegally into the United States anymore," Maria Sandoval went on. "These heartless criminals are now guilty of manslaughter!"

Chapter

Twenty

"**M**ANSLAUGHTER?**" Luis stared at Claire, Nancy, and Bess across their round table of the Café Buena Vida, near el Jardín. The girls had just filled him in on Maria Sandoval's terrible news. "Those crooks don't care about anything but making money, do they?" he said disgustedly.

"That's for sure," Bess agreed. "I mean, all those passengers paid money to get across the border, and the driver just left them to die!"

Luis's face grew red with anger. "The people who do this have no conscience. I gave them five hundred dollars that I will never see again. I cannot believe I trusted them! If I ever get my hands on them—"

"We don't need to do anything rash," Nancy cut

in. She didn't blame him for being angry, but bashing heads wasn't going to put these criminals behind bars.

Claire grimaced at the coffee, rolls, and fruit that were on the table in front of them. "Thinking about it makes me sick. I don't think I can eat."

Nancy felt the same way. "Obviously, the criminals we're up against don't think that human lives are worth anything," she said angrily. "We've got to catch them soon before they hurt someone else."

"Maria Sandoval did warn us again to stay off the case," Claire reminded Nancy. "The ringleaders are very dangerous people if they'll stoop this low."

"That's why I want to make sure they go to jail," Nancy said determinedly. "I'll understand if you guys don't want to help, but—"

"Don't even say it," Bess interrupted. "You know you can count me in."

"Me, too," Claire added. "I have my sculpture class this morning, but after that I'm free."

Luis reached over to take Claire's hand. "You don't think I would let my girlfriend get in trouble alone, do you? I will help also, after my class this morning."

"Great. The first thing I want to do is visit Sam Breslin's studio," Nancy said. "If he's teaching your class, Claire, then we can be sure he won't interrupt us."

"Hey, isn't today Tuesday?" Bess asked. "That's the day the Rápidex truck is supposed to come for his sculpture, right?"

Nancy snapped her fingers. "That's right! We'd

better get up there pronto before the truck arrives. Where should we go, Claire?"

Claire wrote down the directions to the studio. "It's north of town, on the way to the hot springs. You'll have until at least twelve-thirty—that's when class ends. Actually, I'd better get going if I want to be on time." She grinned at everyone around the table. "Luis and I will meet you at the cantina afterward, okay? Good luck!"

"I don't understand where Joe is," Frank said to Ricardo. "He was supposed to come with us."

Ricardo shrugged. "Maybe he went somewhere with Rosa. She was also gone when we got up."

"I don't know why he didn't leave a note, then," Frank said.

For the last hour or so, the two young men had been standing in the shade of a doorway across the street from the Casa Sierra Nevada. Even if Joe had gone out for breakfast or something, Frank was sure he'd have met them by now. What was going on?

"If he ever gets here, I'm going to—" Frank suddenly broke off, his eyes focused on Quentin Cole, who had just appeared on the sidewalk outside the hotel. "There's Cole," he whispered to Ricardo. He ducked into the recess of the doorway until he saw that Cole was heading down the street in the other direction, a newspaper tucked under his arm. Then Frank said to Ricardo in a low voice, "Come on. Let's follow him."

Frank and Ricardo kept as far back as they could

without losing sight of Cole. The tall art collector sauntered casually up the hill to el Jardín, where he sat and read the paper.

"So far, this does not seem suspicious," Ricardo said after half an hour. He and Frank were standing in an arched arcade across the street from the square.

"Stakeouts aren't always as exciting as they seem in the movies. Usually there's a lot of boring waiting around," Frank pointed out.

"Look!" Ricardo said, nodding back at the square. "He is getting up."

This time, Cole took off on a road heading north. "This road leads out of town," Ricardo said. "It goes past the hot springs at Taboada, but he could not possibly walk that far—it's eight kilometers. He must be going someplace closer."

Frank nodded. He detected a new determination in Cole's stride. "I know you're up to something," Frank said under his breath. "And this time I'm going to stick to you like glue."

"Well, this is it." Nancy looked up from the napkin with Claire's scrawled directions on it and stopped in front of a flower-draped fence with a gate in it. "Thirty-eight Calzada de la Luz."

"It's kind of a long walk, but it's worth it," Bess said. "The view from up here is great!"

Nancy had to agree. The red-tiled roofs, stucco houses, trees, and church spires of San Miguel de Allende were spread out below them like a picture postcard. To the west the land flattened to scruffy plains punctuated by ranches.

"We're not here to check out the view, though," she reminded Bess. She pointed to the low stucco building that was visible beyond the bougainvillea-covered fence. "I guess that's Sam Breslin's studio. I see some sculptures outside."

The girls went through the gate and past half a dozen abstract sculptures that were about twelve feet high. A sliding wooden door covered the studio's wide doorway, and crude wooden shutters were closed over the windows.

"I don't see a blue Rápidex truck anywhere," Bess said, gazing around nervously. "I hope it doesn't arrive while we're here."

"The truck's probably not due to get here until after Breslin's class," Nancy said. She frowned at the padlock on the sliding door, then went over to the closest window. Squinting through a wide crack between the shutter's two sides, Nancy saw that they were closed with a simple metal hook. All she had to do was flick up the hook with her finger, and the shutter swung open.

"I guess he's not too worried about security." Nancy grinned over her shoulder, then climbed through the window and jumped lightly to the cement floor inside. Bess clambered through after her.

The studio was one big room about thirty feet long, Nancy saw. The half in which they were standing held materials—piles of wood and large sheets of metal on the floor, and bags of plaster, jars of paint, tarps, tools, and other items on metal shelves against the wall. At the other end of the room was a blowtorch. A table with a few tools on it stood next to an open work area that held only one piece, a towering sculpture that vaguely resembled a person.

"I don't see many sculptures. Maybe Sam was telling the truth about why he used all those Rápidex trucks," Bess said. "But look at this kiln—it's huge!"

Bess had stopped next to a kiln the size of a walk-in closet, with heat controls and a lock outside the door.

"I guess he needs a big kiln to fire the large clay pieces he uses in his sculptures," Nancy said. "The clay oval in that sculpture over there is almost as tall as I am."

She stepped past the kiln and pointed at it. She wasn't sure what the sculpture was supposed to represent, but its geometric shapes were made out of bronze, clay, metal wire, and even pieces taken from old rubber tires.

"I see what Sam meant about using everything but the kitchen sink," Bess said.

Nancy laughed. She headed toward the sculpture in the open work area. "This must be what he's trucking to the States for his show. Here are the silver fish that Luis made for him. And that wooden crate must be what he's going to pack it in."

The bulk of the ten-foot-high piece consisted of a huge fired-clay torso and legs. Sam had used the silver fish and other metal pieces to decorate the clay figure, which stood on spindly metal feet. A twist of copper above the torso suggested a head.

"That's kind of cool," Bess said, gazing up at the sculpture. "I like the way—"

"Bess, check this out," Nancy interrupted, pointing at the hand-shaped tin ornaments that were affixed to the clay legs. "These ornaments are identical to the one Frank and Joe showed us. They're exactly like the one the Hardys found in the gallery after the jade mask was stolen!"

Bess's mouth fell open. "You're right!" she exclaimed. "Wait a second—I don't get it. Why does Sam Breslin have them? Are you trying to say that *he* stole the mask?"

"I'm not sure, but we have to consider it." Nancy said, her mind spinning. "He was in Mexico City at the time of the theft—he told us that he was going there to get materials for his sculpture, remember? And the company that makes the hand ornaments told Frank and Joe they had only one buyer of those particular ones recently—an Anglo. We all thought it was Quentin Cole, but it could have been Sam."

Bess stared up at the sculpture in amazement. "Do you think that somehow Quentin Cole figured out that Sam stole the mask? I mean, maybe that's why he's in San Miguel."

"To steal the mask from Sam!" Nancy finished excitedly. "We'd better get Frank and Joe up here right away."

The girls found a phone on the worktable, and Nancy quickly dialed the Perelises' number. She was relieved when Joe answered the phone. After hearing her news, he promised to join them at the studio.

"Frank and Ricardo are staking out Quentin Cole's hotel, but Joe's on his way over," Nancy explained after she'd hung up. "Let's keep looking around while we're waiting. We can't know for sure that Sam stole the mask until we find it. And we're here to find out if he's sneaking people into the U.S."

For the next fifteen minutes, she and Bess pawed through the shelves, tables, and piles of materials. Nancy was just about to check the shelf of glazes, when Joe's familiar voice called out.

"Hello?"

Nancy saw his head and shoulders framed by the open window. "Hop on in," she invited.

When she and Bess showed him the hand-shaped ornaments on the sculpture, Joe paled. "They're the same ones, all right," he said. "The question is, where's the jade mask?"

"Bess and I already gave this place a pretty good once-over, but we didn't find anything," Nancy told him.

Joe leaned back against the worktable and crossed his arms over his chest. "We've got to think this thing through," he said. "If this guy Breslin *did* steal the mask, he either wants to keep it for himself or sell it to someone—maybe a wealthy collector who doesn't care about breaking the law."

"Do you think he could have sold it already?" Bess asked.

"We have to hope not," Joe said. *"And* we have to hope that Quentin Cole hasn't gotten to the mask ahead of us."

"So the next question is—how can Sam transport the mask to his buyer?" Nancy asked.

As soon as she asked the question, an answer came to her. "Rápidex!" she exclaimed. "Sam arranged for a truck to take his sculpture to the States, and it's coming today!"

Joe went over to the huge wooden crate next to the sculpture. "Maybe Breslin plans to hide the mask in here somewhere."

He looked into the empty crate, then suddenly straightened and stared at something on the outside of the crate.

"What is it, Joe?" Bess asked.

He pointed to the shipping label. "This is the same address we found written on the matchbook in Ramirez's locker—Five Star Gallery, 4753 La Gama Drive. I don't know why they'd both have it, unless—"

"Unless that's where they're sending the jade mask!" Nancy finished excitedly. "The mask has to be here somewhere."

Her eyes fell on the sculpture of the figure at the same time as Joe's. "Are you thinking what I'm thinking?" he asked.

"That the jade mask is somewhere in this thing?" Nancy asked, then shook her head. "It can't be inside the metal, and I don't think Sam would fire a priceless mask inside the clay torso. The extreme heat of the kiln could damage it. But maybe—"

She bent close to the clay torso, examining the bumps and cavities. Along one side, she found what she was searching for. "Yes!" she crowed. "There's a seam. This is actually two pieces of clay. They could have been fired in the kiln and then glued together afterward with the mask inside."

"You're not really going to smash it?" Bess asked, horrified, as Joe picked up a heavy hammer from the worktable. "What if we're wrong and the mask *isn't* there?"

"We'll cross that bridge when we come to it," Joe said.

Nancy and Bess hovered next to the sculpture as Joe tapped the hammer against the clay torso. At first small crack lines appeared in the clay. Then all at once a huge piece of the torso crumbled inward, leaving a hole the size of a basketball. Nancy peered in—and gasped.

"Wow!" Bess said, gazing over Nancy's shoulder into the hole.

There inside the torso, partially covered with bits of clay, was a jade mask in the shape of a monkey. Nancy was overwhelmed by the exceptional beauty and craftsmanship of the piece.

For a long moment the three of them simply stared at the mask. Then Joe turned to Nancy and Bess with a grin. "Looks like we found the goods, folks. Let's call the cops and—"

"I wouldn't do that if I were you," a steely voice spoke up from the studio's open window.

Nancy whirled around. The first thing she saw was the pistol pointing at her, Joe, and Bess. Sam Breslin was holding it. There was a coldness about him that made Nancy shiver.

Bess's hand flew to her mouth. "I thought he was supposed to be in class!" she whispered.

Sam heard her. "I only stayed long enough to demonstrate a special welding technique. Then I had my assistant take over so that I could be here when Rápidex arrives to pick up my sculpture."

"You mean, the mask you stole," Joe said. As

Sam hopped through the window, Nancy saw Joe start to move, but the sculptor whipped his pistol around to level it at Joe.

"Bad move," Sam said. "I don't know which Hardy you are, but both of you have been more trouble than you're worth."

"Coming from you, that's a compliment," Joe said.

Sam shook his head as he turned to Nancy and Bess. "I'm disappointed to see you two here. I hate to have to kill Claire's friends. She's a nice girl."

"K-kill?" Bess asked, the word coming out in a high squeak.

"Afraid so," the sculptor said. He tightened his grip on the pistol and waved Nancy, Bess, and Joe toward the huge kiln. "In there—now," he ordered.

Nancy's blood went cold when she realized what the sculptor intended to do. She looked around frantically as they were herded inside the kiln, but with the gun pointed at them, there wasn't much she could do.

"You won't get away with this," she said, trying to stall for time. "Claire knows where we are. She'll call the police when we don't return."

"I'll be long gone with the jade mask by then," Sam said. "Now, you'd better take a good look around, because what you see is the last thing you'll see in your life."

Nancy caught a brief glimpse of bougainvillea outside the studio window. Then the kiln door slammed shut.

Chapter

Twenty-One

"I DON'T LIKE THIS," Frank whispered to Ricardo. "Cole has been standing there for a while now. Why doesn't he *do* something?"

Ricardo looked at him and shrugged, keeping low behind the bougainvillea-covered fence. The two had followed the art collector to this low stucco building north of San Miguel. It looked as if he was going to sneak into the building, but when he'd approached the only open window, Cole stopped short and flattened himself against the wall next to the window, where he couldn't be seen from inside. Even from this distance, Frank could see Cole's frown.

"Let's move farther down the fence," Frank suggested. "I want to get a look in that window."

Frank crept to the right about twenty feet, then

poked his head above the fence again. From there he could just see through the window and—

"Nancy, Joe, and Bess are in there!" he whispered to Ricardo. "A guy's got a gun on them!"

"A gun?" Ricardo's face went tight as he stood up just enough to see over the fence. "He is locking them into a big box. What if he shoots them? We have to do something!"

Frank peeked again and saw the tall, brown-haired man close the door and start fiddling with some kind of dial. "I'm not sure what that is, but it looks like bad news," he muttered. "Come on!"

Quentin Cole was still keeping watch just outside the window, but Frank couldn't worry about him. They had to get inside that building fast!

Frank and Ricardo hopped over the fence and ran toward the open window in a low crouch. Cole's eyes widened when he caught sight of them, and Frank put a warning finger to his lips. To his amazement, Quentin Cole nodded and gave him a thumbs-up sign. As Frank and Ricardo drew closer to the building, Cole circled around the side of the building.

Taking another glance in the window, Frank saw that the tall man had put his pistol down on a worktable and was adjusting the dial outside the huge closet. It looked like a thermostat—

Whoa! That's no closet—it's a kiln! he realized. This guy's going to roast Nancy, Joe, and Bess!

"We need to find a way to distract him," he mouthed to Ricardo. "Otherwise, we don't have a chance of getting inside."

No sooner were the words out of his mouth, than

he heard a rapping noise coming from the other side of the studio.

"What? Who's there!" The man inside jumped away from the kiln, grabbed the pistol, and charged toward the noise.

"Now!" Frank whispered, and vaulted through the window. It took only a split second for the man to realize he was there. Frank saw the gun whirl in his direction. He dove for the table by the window, knocking it over to use as a shield just before the man hit the trigger.

Blam! Blam!

The noise was deafening. Frank saw that two holes had been blasted in the table over his head. He didn't see Ricardo, so he guessed he was still outside.

"Ricardo! Stay down!" Frank called out. Just then, another tapping noise sounded from the opposite wall. Frank glanced over the table's edge to see the man turn in the direction of the noise.

That moment was all the time Frank needed. He grabbed a metal bar that had fallen from the table and hurled it at the man's gun hand. The bar slammed into his arm, sending the gun flying.

"Ow!" The man fell to the ground, clutching his arm. Frank jumped over the table and was on the guy in a second, pinning him to the ground.

Moments later Quentin Cole jumped into the room through the window where the tapping had come from. Cole picked up the pistol and pointed it at Breslin's head. Ricardo was now inside, too, and hurried to unlock the huge kiln.

Nancy, Bess, and Joe stumbled out.

"Boy, are we glad to see you!" Bess exclaimed, rushing into Ricardo's arms.

"I'll say," Nancy added, hugging Frank.

Frank noticed the way Joe's eyes narrowed when he saw Quentin Cole holding the pistol on Breslin. "I'll take that," Joe said, holding out his hand.

A knot twisted in Frank's gut when he saw Cole hesitate. Then, with a sigh, Cole handed over the pistol. "As you like."

There was a look of genuine appreciation in the collector's eyes as he gazed into the cavity in the sculpture's torso. Frank walked over to see what Cole was so interested in. "The jade mask!"

Nancy nodded. "We're pretty sure Sam Breslin stole it," she said.

While Ricardo called the police and his father, Frank found some rope and tied Breslin's hands behind his back. Nancy, Joe, and Bess filled him in on how they'd discovered the mask.

"You were pretty tricky, Breslin," Frank said to the sculptor. "I guess you figured that by leaving that hand ornament in the gallery, the police would suspect Quentin Cole."

Breslin struggled against his ropes but said nothing.

"You must have heard about the thief leaving a hand behind at other big thefts and that Cole was a suspect," Nancy put in.

"You kids have it all figured out, don't you?" Breslin said disdainfully.

"Ramirez was in it, too, just as we thought." Joe pulled Frank over to the packing crate, and Frank let out a low whistle when he read the address.

"The same one we found on that matchbook Ramirez had. What's the story, Breslin? Is your buyer hooked into that gallery?" Seeing the sculptor hesitate, Frank added, "You might as well tell us everything. The police might go easier on you."

Breslin's eyes flashed with fury. Then, suddenly, all the fight seemed to go out of him. "It was the perfect plan," he finally said. "Ramirez is the one who was approached by a very rich, eccentric art collector. The guy is crazy for pre-Columbian art, and he wanted the mask—badly enough to offer a lot of money to anyone who could get it for him."

"But why would Juan betray my father that way?" Ricardo asked indignantly. He was standing beside Bess, one arm around her protectively.

Sam shrugged. "I guess he saw your dad getting rich from his business, and he decided he deserved a piece of the action," he said. "Juan told me the collector approached him after overhearing him argue with Perelis about a raise. I guess the collector figured Juan might be disgruntled enough to steal from his boss."

"I don't get it. How did *you* get involved?" Bess asked.

"Years ago, when I first came to Mexico, I had a summer job helping out in a gallery in Mexico City," Breslin said. "Ramirez was a guard there, and he and I became friendly. Anyway, one time, a sculpture that I was crazy about came into the gallery."

"Let me guess," Joe said, coming to stand in front of Sam Breslin. "You helped yourself to it."

"I just wanted to borrow it for a night so I could

study it and try to copy it. Juan helped me to sneak it out of the gallery and get it back in the next morning before anyone else knew it was missing," the sculptor said. "It worked so well that we did the same thing a half dozen other times."

"And naturally, when Juan needed someone to help steal the jade mask, he thought of you," she said disgustedly.

Breslin nodded. "I was waiting when Juan arrived for the morning shift. As soon as the night guard left, Juan turned off the alarm to let me in. Then we opened the case so I could take the mask."

"So the two of you left that tin ornament and faked Ramirez getting knocked out just to throw the cops off the track," Frank guessed.

"I guess Ramirez wasn't happy when he realized Frank and Joe suspected him anyway," Bess put in.

Breslin let out his breath in a long sigh. "He called to warn me that you two were on the case. I figured the threatening call I made to you at the gallery would be enough to convince a couple of kids to back off."

"You figured wrong. And Ramirez figured wrong when he attacked us at the bazaar and the floating gardens," Joe said. "That *was* him, right?"

The sculptor nodded. Quentin Cole had been listening to the explanation in silence, his expression impassive. Now, for the first time, he spoke up.

"The bottom line seems to be that you've been caught, my dear fellow," Cole said. "One would think that you'd know better than to imitate the experts. Such a shoddy plan is an insult to"—he hesitated briefly before saying—"them."

Frank was sure he'd been about to say "us."

"Shoddy!" Breslin objected. "Our plan was perfect! I was going to ship the mask inside the sculpture to my gallery in L.A. Then, the collector who wanted the mask was going to buy the sculpture—"

"With the mask inside," Frank finished. Turning to Quentin Cole, he said, "I'm curious. How did you know that Breslin and Ramirez pulled this theft?"

Cole hesitated, and Frank had the feeling that he was deciding how much information to divulge. "I don't see why you would think I *knew* anything," Cole began. "It's a simple matter to deduce that this was an inside job. If one were diligent in observing the gallery's employees, one might well be lucky enough to witness a meeting between one of those employees and his accomplice."

"I get the idea," Frank said. His head was starting to hurt from trying to follow Cole's vague explanation. Just then he heard the sounds of approaching sirens.

"Well, it looks as if your perfect plan has been changed," Joe said. "You'll have to make new arrangements—to spend a lot of time behind bars."

"I'd like to make a toast," Claire said an hour and a half later, raising her glass of soda. "Here's to the Hardys' case being solved."

"And to Nancy, Joe, and Bess escaping from that kiln," Luis added.

After giving their statements to the police, Nancy, Bess, the Hardys, Ricardo, Claire, and Luis had decided to celebrate with lunch at the institute's cantina. Mr. Oberman had been able to confirm for the police that the mask was a genuine pre-Columbian piece, and Ricardo's father was on his way from Mexico City to make definite identification. The police in Mexico City had already picked up Juan Ramirez. Everything was in order.

Except for tracking down the people who were responsible for ferrying Mexicans into the U.S.

Nancy let out a sigh. Now that Sam Breslin was no longer a suspect in her case and their stakeout at the church had been botched, Nancy wasn't sure where to go with her investigation. To make matters worse, the academic panel had arrived in San Miguel that morning, and Nancy knew that Mr. and Mrs. Oberman wouldn't be able to relax for a second. Even though the Obermans had asked her to back off the case, Nancy felt as if she had let them down.

"Would you like anything else?" Ana Perón's soft voice broke into Nancy's thoughts. After writing down their orders for more soft drinks, Ana started to walk away, but Nancy held her back.

"We heard some sad news this morning," Nancy said. She went on to tell the waitress about the Rápidex truck crash near the border. "Two people were killed, Ana," she finished, "and the police are pretty sure that the criminals responsible are working right here in San Miguel."

Ana just stood there, staring at Nancy in total dismay. "Two people—dead?" she finally whispered. "It cannot be true!"

"It is," Bess said soberly. "Ana, if you know—"

Suddenly Ana hid her face in her hands and started crying. "It is too terrible. I cannot lie anymore."

Nancy placed her hand gently on the girl's arm. "If you know anything about these people, you have to tell us. It could help save lives."

Ana took a few deep breaths and wiped the tears from her cheeks. "A few weeks ago, when I first learned that my brother was sick, I paid money to be taken across the border to the United States," she began, her voice barely above a whisper.

The whole table had quieted down, Nancy realized, and they were all listening to Ana. "I could tell you recognized the telephone number I had here the other day," Nancy said. "Was that the number of your contact?"

Ana nodded. "When I saw it I was terrified! I did not know why you were asking me all those questions about going to the U.S., but I was afraid to tell you the truth. I do not want to go to jail—I just want to live with my brother!"

"Maybe you'd better tell us everything that happened, from the beginning," Frank suggested.

"Very well." Ana took a deep breath. "My brother gave me the telephone number. I do not know the name of the person I spoke to when I called, but he told me to bring my money to the Finca Mendoza. It is a"—she paused, looking at Ricardo—*"finca de vacas."*

"Cattle ranch," Luis supplied. "There are a lot of them on the plains between here and Guanajuato."

Nancy nodded, making a mental note of the

name of the ranch. "Six other people were there, too," Ana went on. "We were taken north in a truck—"

"A blue truck, with an *R* on it?" Bess cut in.

"Yes," Ana replied. "There was a false panel in the truck, and we had to hide behind that. It was such a long ride, and so hot—I thought I would suffocate!"

"Obviously your health wasn't very important to the driver," Claire commented.

"*Sí.* I know that now," Ana said. "When we got close to the border the driver stopped and made us get out. He told us that it was too dangerous to cross in the truck. Instead, he pointed out a path through the woods." She shook with anger as she relived the trip. "He did not even come with us, and of course the border patrol caught us and sent us back."

Nancy noticed Luis's jaw tighten as Ana told her story. "They cheated me, too. It is hard to believe that people can treat other human beings this way," he said.

"Now I have no more money," Ana went on, tears brimming in her eyes again. "I have not heard from Ernesto in over a week, and I am afraid that his illness is worse. I do not like to break the law, but I must find a way to go to him! I must be able to work and take care of him."

Nancy's heart went out to the girl. "I called my father last night, and he's checking out ways to help you," she told Ana.

Ana blinked back her tears. "It is too good to be true. I am very grateful to you."

"But in the meantime, it's very important that

you tell us *anything* you can think of that might help us find the people who are behind this ring," Nancy went on.

Ana's brow furrowed. "The man who drove the truck was short and skinny. I did not learn his name."

Hmm, Nancy thought. The driver didn't sound like that burly man with the crooked nose. But that wasn't surprising—in a ring this large, there had to be more than one person driving the trucks.

"Oh!" Ana said. "There is one more thing."

"What is it?" Claire asked.

"The second time I called the number, I overheard something. The person put his hand over the phone to talk to someone else, but I could still hear him. I heard him call the other person el Conejo."

She started as some people at a table across the cantina called to her. "Oh—I must go. I am sorry I did not help you more."

"El Conejo?" Luis repeated after Ana hurried away. "That means 'the rabbit.' Sounds like a nickname."

Suddenly Joe sat bolt upright in his chair. "Wait a second—I think I know who el Conejo is!"

Nancy was surprised. "You're kidding! Who?"

"I overheard Rosa talking to him this morning," Joe said excitedly. "El Conejo is none other than her boyfriend, Jim Stanton."

Chapter

Twenty-Two

FRANK'S JAW DROPPED. "Jim Stanton? Are you *sure?*" Checking the faces around the table, he saw that the others were as surprised as he was.

"Positive," Joe answered. "I followed Rosa to his place this morning. They started arguing so I didn't stick around, but before I left, I heard her call him el Conejo. He got really mad and said never to call him that. I guess we know why now."

"Hey! I just realized something else, too," Nancy exclaimed. "Claire, remember all the initials of coyotes in the book we found at Rápidex? The initials *EC* were all over the place."

Claire leaned forward excitedly in her chair. "That's right! I bet they stand for *el Conejo.*"

"Qué terrible," Ricardo said. "I must warn her." He jumped up, but Frank held him back.

199

"Wait! We have to think of a way to make sure Rosa's safe without letting Stanton know we're onto him," he warned. "Otherwise, he could get away."

Ricardo frowned darkly. "I will phone him," he decided. "If she isn't there, I will try our house."

"Good idea," Nancy agreed. "But if she's at Stanton's house, make up some excuse to get her out of there that won't make him suspicious."

Ricardo nodded, then went to the counter, where he consulted a phone book. After making a call from the pay phone, he returned to the table. "There was no answer at Jim's apartment, but luckily Rosa is at home." He was obviously relieved. "I'm going there right away to talk to her."

"Make sure you make her promise to keep this quiet," Frank reminded Ricardo.

As soon as he was gone, Nancy turned to the others and said, "If Stanton's not at his place, I think we should go check it out."

"Yes. I want to help catch the person who has ruined so many lives," Luis said, his dark eyes flashing angrily. "I was a fool to ever contact such criminals! If I get my hands on him—"

"Whoa!" Joe said, grabbing Luis's arm. "I know how you feel, but once we get the goods on Stanton, we'll have to leave the rest to the police."

Nancy knew they were taking a chance by going after Stanton on their own. If Maria Sandoval found out, they would be in big trouble, but Nancy didn't see the detective anywhere at the cantina, and they couldn't afford to wait. After paying their check, she, Frank, Bess, Joe, Claire, and Luis were off.

It took only ten minutes to reach Jim Stanton's apartment building. "There are too many of us," Nancy said, pausing outside the door. "We can't all go in."

"I'll keep watch out here and head Stanton off if he shows up," Bess offered.

"Luis and I will keep you company," Claire said. Nancy could tell that Luis wanted to go inside, but he reluctantly agreed with Claire.

Nancy's heart raced as she and Frank followed Joe around the deserted courtyard to a door on the right. She rapped firmly on the door. "If he answers, we'll say we're looking for Rosa," she whispered.

"We're in luck," Frank said, when no one came to the door. He took his credit card from his wallet and worked it into the crack between the door and the doorjamb. A moment later the lock clicked open, and the door swung inward.

Stepping inside, Nancy found herself in a room that doubled as the living room and kitchen. A worn couch and two chairs stood on a woven rug to the right of the door. To the left was a red wooden table and chairs. A hot plate stood on the counter. Through an open doorway, Nancy saw what looked like a studio, with an easel, paints, and canvases. A bed with a striped Mexican blanket over it was squeezed into one corner, and a dresser was next to it.

"Mmm," she said, going into the studio. She ran

a finger carefully over the painting on the easel. "Stanton is supposed to be a painter, but this painting is covered with dust. And the paint on his palette is cracked and dried up."

"If Stanton *is* el Conejo, then he's been way too busy breaking the law to have time for painting," Frank called through the doorway.

"We still have to prove that," Nancy said. "You guys search in there. I'll take this room."

She shuffled through some papers on top of the dresser but found only some old bills. Her search of the drawers didn't turn up anything unusual, either, so she headed for the bed.

"Any luck, Nan?" Frank called just as she finished feeling beneath the mattress.

Nancy sighed and got to her feet. "Not yet." She started walking toward the easel, then paused as one of the floorboards next to the bed gave way slightly, letting out a loud squeak.

"Hmm, I wonder if—" She dropped quickly to her knees. The floorboard was only about a foot long, and when Nancy tapped her knuckles against it, she heard a hollow sound.

"You guys, I think I found something!" she called to Frank and Joe. Nancy dug at the edge of the board with her fingertips, trying to pry it out. Frank and Joe both appeared next to her just as she lifted up one corner of the board, revealing a hole about a foot deep and four inches wide.

Nancy's pulse raced when she saw the half dozen stacks of pale pink cards resting at the bottom of the cavity. Even before she spotted the blue U.S. Immigration seal printed on them, she knew what they were. "Blank green cards," she said, flipping through the stack. "There must be hundreds of them!"

"I guess business is booming," Joe said, shaking his head in disgust.

Frank dropped to the floor and grabbed a small notebook next to the cards, then opened it. "Hey— there are a bunch of names and phone numbers here."

"Looks like a list of the other people in the ring. This is definitely going to make the police work a lot easier!" Nancy said, grinning. She looked over Frank's shoulder as he flipped through the notebook. "And these next pages contain some kind of records. There's a separate page for every month," she murmured, reading the scrawled notations: "'Green cards sold—fifty-five' . . ."

Joe let out a low whistle. "At a thousand bucks a pop, that's a lot of money!"

"And that was just for March," Frank put in.

Nancy's attention was so completely focused on the record book that she barely heard the Hardys. "'Passengers—one hundred and twenty-five in ten trucks,'" she continued to read. "And down here it gives the total amount of money taken in for the month." She glanced at the figure, then gaped at Frank and Joe. "He made almost a hundred thousand dollars!"

"I'll say one thing for the guy. He sure keeps good records. Check this out," Frank said. He pointed to a list of dates to the right of the figures. "This looks like a list of when and where the truckloads of passengers left."

"You're right!" Nancy realized. She took the book from Frank and flipped to the last page. "Here are the records for this month so far." Her gaze flew down to the list of truck rendezvous points. When she came to the last entry, she gasped.

"You guys, this rendezvous is for today!" she exclaimed, showing the entry to Frank and Joe.

Joe bent to look at the entry. "Finca Mendoza," he read. "Two-thirty P.M." He glanced at his watch, then jolted to attention. "That's in half an hour!"

Nancy hastily gathered up the immigration cards and the notebook and stuffed them in her shoulder bag. "I want to call Maria Sandoval and tell her we have this stuff. Then we'd better find out where that ranch is and get there right away!"

After replacing the floorboard, Nancy, Joe, and Frank hurried out to the street and told Claire, Luis, and Bess what they had found.

"I'm pretty sure the Finca Mendoza is west of San Miguel, off the same road that goes to the train and bus stations," Claire said, turning to her boyfriend. "You know the place I mean?"

Luis didn't answer but simply stood there glowering. As Nancy watched, his face became mottled with rage.

"What an evil person!" Luis finally burst out. "I have only met Jim Stanton one time, but when I see him again . . ." He jabbed the air with his fists.

"Calm down," Claire said, putting an arm around Luis's shoulders, but he shook her away.

"I can't calm down," Luis said. "He is giving a bad name to all the honest people who come to live and work here in San Miguel."

Nancy was worried. She didn't want Luis's hot temper to get in the way of what could be a dangerous situation out at the cattle ranch. "Um, Claire, I think you and Luis should call the police and tell Maria Sandoval what's happening. Tell her that Bess, Frank, Joe, and I will wait for them outside the ranch."

Claire nodded. "My parents have one of the cars, but you can use the other," she told Nancy. "The keys are on a hook in the kitchen."

Luis acted as if he were going to object, but he grudgingly allowed Claire to lead him down the street. Nancy followed them with her eyes for a moment before turning to her friends. "Let's go!"

Joe, Bess, Frank, and Nancy crouched in the shadow of a juniper tree and stared at the low buildings of the Finca Mendoza, several hundred yards away. The dusty brown buildings echoed the earthy tones of the dry plains, where cattle were grazing.

Luckily, the road leading to the ranch ran along a small ridge. Joe didn't think anyone could have seen the Obermans' car approaching. They had pulled off the road and parked by some scruffy bushes outside the barbed wire fence to the ranch. Then they had crept under the barbed wire and hid in the junipers. They had brought a pair of binoculars from Claire's house, and now Nancy was gazing intently through them.

"Do you see anything, Nancy?" Bess asked.

Nancy lowered out the binoculars and leveled a serious look at the others. "The Rápidex truck is already there! At least a dozen people are waiting by it."

She held out the binoculars to Joe. Peering through the lenses, he spotted the rear of a blue truck sticking out from behind a barn. A man was standing there, gesturing for a group of men and women to get into the truck.

"Hey, that's our friend with the broken nose," Joe commented. He lowered the binoculars and stood up. "I don't see Stanton anywhere, but I don't think we should wait for him to show up. That truck could be long gone before the police get here!"

Joe noticed the tight set of Frank's jaw as he scrutinized the grazing land between them and the ranch. "That's a pretty open stretch. We'll have to use the cattle as cover," Frank said.

"What!" Bess tugged nervously at her T-shirt, eyeing a group of cattle a dozen feet away. "How can we be sure they won't stampede or something?"

"They seem pretty tame," Nancy said. "We have to risk it, and we don't have any time to lose!"

Nancy took the lead, followed by Frank and Bess, with Joe bringing up the rear. As they came close to the first group of cattle, a few of them snorted and moved restlessly.

"Hurry up!" Bess urged. "I don't like the way these beasts are looking at us!"

"Nice cow," Joe murmured, but he was moving as quickly as he could, too. He was relieved when they finally reached a wooden gate near the barn where the Rápidex truck was. Joe couldn't see the truck from where they were, but he could hear voices speaking in Spanish around the corner of the barn.

He froze when he heard the *thunk* of the truck's metal door closing. Nancy shot an urgent glance at him, Bess, and Frank. "Let's go," she mouthed.

Moving quickly and stealthily, the four of them climbed over the wooden fence and ran to the barn. There was an open doorway on the side facing them, and the teens ducked inside and crouched behind a row of cattle stalls. Through a large, open sliding wooden door on the other side of the barn, Joe could clearly see the blue truck and the stocky man with the crooked nose. He was walking toward the driver's door. Joe guessed that the other people were already hidden inside the truck.

"It looks as if he's alone," Nancy whispered as they crept toward the sliding door.

"Which means it's four to one in our favor," Frank whispered back, grinning. "Piece of cake."

Adrenaline pumped through Joe. He could tell that the others were also primed and ready to go. When they reached the open doorway, Nancy gave a quick nod, and they sprang into action.

Frank leapt forward, grabbing the guy by the shirt and pulling him away from the truck. The man reached for Frank's throat, but Nancy hit him with a judo kick that knocked him to the ground. A second later Joe had the man's arms pinned behind his back while Frank sat on the man's legs.

"Easy, guy," Joe said through gritted teeth.

"Could you guys use this?" Bess called out from the doorway of the barn. Joe saw that she was holding up a coil of heavy rope.

"Definitely." Joe was reaching out to take the rope, when a deep voice growled at him from somewhere near the front of the truck.

"Hold it right there, all of you!"

Joe jerked around to see Jim Stanton coming out of an outbuilding next to the barn, holding a gun. Joe froze when he saw that Stanton wasn't alone. He roughly herded two people in front of him, keeping his gun trained on them.

"Claire! Luis!" Nancy exclaimed with a gasp. "What are *you* doing here?"

Chapter

Twenty-Three

NANCY FELT her stomach churn as she stared at the gun Jim Stanton had trained on Claire and Luis. Claire was visibly shaking, but Luis's face was a dark mask of anger. She knew they couldn't risk trying to overpower Stanton—the consequences could be too deadly.

"What these two *intended* to do doesn't matter anymore," Jim Stanton said, his angular features cold and impassive. "I have different plans."

He gestured for Frank and Joe to release the stocky man. "What kind of plans?" Joe asked.

There was an evil glint in Stanton's eyes as he said, "You know what they say about dead men telling no tales—" he began.

"You can't just kill us in cold blood!" Bess squeaked out.

"Why not?" Stanton countered. "There are lots of places to hide the evidence on a big ranch like this, and I pay Señor Mendoza enough money to stay out of the way and keep his mouth shut." He shoved Claire and Luis over toward Nancy, Bess, and the Hardys, then nodded toward the stocky man. "Jorge, take that rope and tie them up."

Jorge made the six of them sit on the ground, back to back in a circle, and then he bound all of their wrists together using the long cord he'd taken from Bess. How were they going to get out of this one! Nancy wondered. And where were the police?

"Sorry, you guys," Claire whispered. "After we left you, Luis was so mad that he insisted on coming here to confront Jim Stanton."

"You two weren't very smart, riding right up here on that moped," Stanton said. "Luis here must think he's the Lone Ranger, the way he tried to jump me. I guess he learned too late that no one tangles with Jim Stanton and gets away with it."

Luis let out a stream of Spanish words and tugged on the rope binding him. As he moved, Nancy felt the rope shift slightly around her wrists. Was it her imagination, or was there a little play in the rope?

"You've got a pretty good setup going here," Frank said. "How'd you get into this business, anyway?"

Nancy knew he was stalling for time. Please, let Stanton fall for it, she begged silently.

Stanton hesitated for a long moment, then chuckled and said, "I guess it can't hurt to tell you, since you won't be around to repeat the story."

Moving as little as possible, Nancy was twisting her hands back and forth behind her back. "I thought you were an artist," she prompted. "What happened?"

"Rosa's father happened," Stanton said. "The day he forbade me to date Rosa was the best day of my life."

"I don't get it," Bess said. "I thought you two were in love."

"Or maybe you were in love with her family's money and art connections, just as Mr. Perelis thought," Joe accused.

Stanton didn't even try to deny it. "I'm a realist. I figured that Mr. Perelis knew the kind of people who could make me famous." He shrugged. "Too bad he wouldn't introduce me to any of them. But he gave me the ticket to a great future anyway, the day he paid me off to stop dating Rosa."

Nancy could hardly believe her ears. Stanton actually sounded proud of his sleazy behavior. "You took money from him?"

The rope around her wrists was loosening a tiny bit more with each twist she gave. She had already worked it down over the backs of her hands. If she could just get it past her knuckles, she'd be free!

"Over five thousand dollars," Stanton said smugly. "I had helped a Mexican friend to get into the U.S. It worked so well that I decided to use my five grand to expand into a real business. That's how I got started helping people to a better future."

"You mean, breaking the law by sneaking people into the States," Frank said.

"Not to mention letting passengers die if you run into any trouble," Claire said disgustedly.

Nancy was sweating from the intensity of her efforts. Just a little more, she thought, and I'll be able to—

Yes!

She had to keep herself from letting out a victory whoop as she felt the rope fall away.

"Think what you want," Stanton said. "All that matters to me is that the people in this truck—and thousands more like them—are willing to pay for my services."

Behind her back, Nancy gave a quick tug on the rope to let Frank know that there was more play in his rope now. He gave a slight nod, and she could feel him going to work on his binds.

"We know you're selling fake green cards, too," Nancy said, trying to keep Stanton distracted. "How did you get them printed?"

"I have friends who were only too happy to print them for a small cut of the action," he answered.

He paused, as a banging sound came from inside the truck. "I see that our passengers are getting restless." He nodded at Jorge, who was lounging in the open doorway of the truck's cabin. "You can get on the road as soon as we take care of our friends here."

Nancy could tell Frank had gotten his hands free, too—and not a moment too soon! Jim Stanton and Jorge were closing in on them.

When Stanton was just a few feet away, Nancy made her move, shooting out her left foot with all her strength.

"Hey!" Stanton yelled as she kicked the gun from his hand and sent it flying underneath the truck.

Out of the corner of her eye, Nancy saw Frank leap forward and smash himself into Jorge. Nancy made a grab for Jim Stanton's wrists, but he managed to twist away.

"I'm right with you!" Joe cried. Shaking his hands free of the rope, he made a dive for Stanton, who was racing for the truck. Joe got hold of the man's ankles, throwing him forward.

Nancy cringed when she heard the painful *thunk* of Stanton's head hitting the side of the truck. Then, he fell limply to the ground.

"He's out cold," Nancy said, jumping to check his pulse while Joe scrambled forward to grab the pistol from beneath the truck. He jumped up and trained it on Jorge, who was still struggling with Frank.

"Give it up, guy," Joe said.

Still breathing hard, Nancy hurried over to help untie Claire, Bess, and Luis. Bess cocked her head to one side as she stood up.

"Do you guys hear that?"

Nancy felt a rush of relief when she heard the faint wail of the police siren. She turned to grin at her friends. "Better late than never!"

"Mmm. This roast pork is delicious!" Bess said that night, licking some spicy marinade from her upper lip. "I was starving!"

"Me, too," Nancy agreed. She grinned around the large table at Bess, Claire, Luis, the Hardys, and Ricardo and Rosa. Mr. and Mrs. Oberman sat at an adjoining table, along with Mr. Perelis and the four men and women who made up the academic review panel. Now that Jim Stanton had been taken into custody and the rounds of police questioning were through, they could all relax. "It's great of your parents to take us all out for dinner," she told Claire.

"They were happy to," Claire said. "You can't believe how relieved they are that no one from the institute is mixed up in selling fake green cards."

"Not to mention that no one got hurt," Nancy added. She glanced at the other table. There was a lively conversation going on, but Nancy noticed the warm looks that the Obermans and Mr. Perelis kept shooting at their children.

"Too bad we didn't have time to stop by the cantina," Bess commented. "I can't wait to give Ana the good news."

"I bet she'll be glad to hear that your dad can help her get the papers she needs to stay in the U.S. legally," Frank said.

Joe sopped up some chicken gravy with a piece of bread, then swallowed it in one bite. "At least Jim Stanton won't be able to hurt anyone else."

Claire nodded. "Maria Sandoval called my parents to say that the evidence you guys found in Stanton's apartment will clinch the case against him. The police are using the record book to round up the other people in his network, too. Apparently, that guy Jorge works for Rápidex, but Stanton bought him off to work as his right-hand man. Jorge was the contact person—he made the meeting arrangement for this area."

Nancy noticed the pained look on Rosa's face at the mention of Stanton. She had been uncharacteristically quiet all evening, and Nancy couldn't help feeling for her. It had to be terrible finding out that she'd been dating a criminal.

"I'm sorry about how things worked out, Rosa," Nancy said gently, but Rosa waved away her words.

"I should have known something was going on," she said. "For the last few months, Jim wasn't being nearly as nice as when I first met him last year. He would never tell me anything about what he was doing."

"But how did you know about his nickname, el Conejo?" Luis asked.

Rosa shrugged. "I overheard someone call him that when we were at a club one night. I guess the music was so loud that he thought I didn't hear." As she spoke, she picked distractedly at her spiced sausage with her fork. "I cannot believe how gullible I was! Suddenly Jim had a lot of money, and I believed him when he said he had sold a painting. He was just pretending to be an artist—just like he was pretending to like me." Rosa glanced over her shoulder at Mr. Perelis, then frowned down at her plate. "Once my father paid Jim off, he didn't have to pretend anymore. I guess I didn't want to admit to myself that Jim didn't care about me. It was easier to think that my father was the problem."

Ricardo leaned over and placed a protective hand on his sister's arm. "It is not all your fault, Rosa. Papa was wrong to offer Jim money behind your back," he told her. "But things will be different now," he explained to the others. "Rosa and I spoke for a long time with our father when he arrived from Mexico City this afternoon. From now on, they will try harder to understand each other."

"I'll have a lot of time to spend with him," Rosa added with a wry smile, "because after this, I don't think I will ever date again."

"Don't say that!" Bess cried, horrified. "I'm sure you'll meet tons of guys who are cuter *and* nicer than Jim Stanton."

"I can think of one person right here, as a matter of fact," Claire added, grinning at Joe.

Joe made a quick bow to Rosa across the table and flashed a quick smile. "At your service."

"If you can forgive him for being so tough on you, that is," Frank added, punching his brother lightly on the shoulder.

Rosa smiled back at the Hardys. "I'm not in the mood for dating, but I wouldn't mind spending time with some good friends."

As Nancy looked around the table, she could feel the warmth that radiated among the group. Her eyes met Frank's. He winked at her and raised his glass.

"Here's to spending time with friends," he toasted.

She held up her glass and smiled warmly at him. "To friends."

THE HARDY BOYS® CASE FILES

Simon & Schuster Mail Order
200 Old Tappan Rd., Old Tappan, N.J. 07675

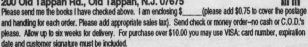

Please send me the books I have checked above. I am enclosing $_____(please add $0.75 to cover the postage and handling for each order. Please add appropriate sales tax). Send check or money order—no cash or C.O.D.'s please. Allow up to six weeks for delivery. For purchase over $10.00 you may use VISA: card number, expiration date and customer signature must be included.

Name _____

Address _____

City _____ State/Zip _____

VISA Card # _____ Exp.Date _____

Signature _____ 762-13